MURMURATION

ELISABETH PIKE

ABOUT THE AUTHOR

Elisabeth Pike is a freelance writer and maker. Her work has been published by The *Guardian, Third Way* and *Oh magazine* amongst others. *Voice at the Window: One hundred gratitude poems written during lockdown* was funded through Kickstarter and is out now. This is her first novel. Find her at elisabethpike.co.uk

Murmuration
A novel

Elisabeth Pike

For my children,
may you always look to the birds.

PROLOGUE

F riday 24th September 2021
   Southend-On-Sea

SHE'S NOT the type to run away, but she was propelled here by an urge so strong she couldn't deny it. All she knew was go south, go east, keep going until you reach the sea.

There was nothing to stay for and every reason to leave.

She watches the birds from the pier at Southend-on-Sea. She shivers and wraps her arms tightly around herself. Her eyes flick down to the pebbly shore where a gang of lads are hurling rocks into the sea.

A handful of starlings are thrown across an empty sky; they fall sideways like dice from a cup. They dive and change course at speed, and yet not one of them collides with another; their flight is finely tuned and crafted to perfection.

She longs to join them with such intensity that her goosebumps sprout feathers and her heart shrinks to a fifth of its size. Her eyes double in their capability and her voice sharpens to a song.

She doesn't know what is happening to her, but she cannot stop it. All she knows is the wanting; to be outside of her skin, to be something she was not before.

She leans forward into the wind and her clothes fall like streamers behind her. She surrenders to the undoing, becomes a small, feathered thing, and takes flight in the silky night.

She is heading for the island; it draws her like magnetism. She is homing, although she has never set foot there before.

There is a reason that she needs to get there, but she isn't sure what it is yet.

$$1$$

JAY

Friday 24th September 2021
Isle of Sheppey

BEFORE

Some days you can almost forget that the world is crumbling. Take your meds, drink until the edges get softer. Look down, think small. Today and then the next.

This new way has melted down around us, dreamlike. We've forgotten what used to make us boil with rage, what used to make us glad. It's like the morning haze out on the marsh, but it won't clear. We can't tell what's real anymore.

Pete still lets us into The Black Dog, only serves us Coke, though. Last crate, he says. £5 a pop. Imagine a world without Coke. It's jokes. While we've still got it, we savour its bite, the way it rushes down your throat, giving you that sweet kick.

Pete rings the bell for last orders and Swanny, Robin and I wander out into the evening. Strangely warm.

'Shall we go up to the lake?' Swanny says.

I shrug, 'May as well, nothing else to do', but my stomach swims as I say it.

The moon lights up the road a little before us. All quiet.

A few starlings loop and dive ahead of us. Their fanned tails snatch my gaze, pull my eyes to the sky.

Not much to say these days. Just this road, just this night, just the scrape of our shoes on the dirt track and the click of the bike wheels turning over and over.

We get to the lake, sit there on the shore. A rowing boat is pulled up on the mud, lashed to a stake in the ground.

A breeze has picked up, and the night seems darker than down in the town. The moon still shines a little, casting a silver hue across the water. No one else around. Funny how claustrophobic it can feel with this much emptiness.

I take a packet of ciggies out of my pocket, offer one each to Swanny and Rob and light one for myself. Went mad, didn't we? Me and Dad, after the Cut Off. Bought all the ciggies we could find. I ration them now, one a day. The bitter taste clears my mind.

Swanny opens his rucksack and pulls out a four-pack of lager, saying, 'Look lads, Pete may not serve us yet, but I feel we need a little engine oil for tonight. A little lubrication.'

'Where d'you get that from?' Robin asks.

Swanny taps the side of his nose, knowingly. 'Wouldn't you like to know?'

'Yeah, I would actually' Robin shoots back, with a glare.

Treats us like kids Swanny does. Pisses us off. Things are thinning out, costing twice as much, so how does he get them? We down the cans and it's never enough but it gives me that warm burn in the pit of my belly, and it fuels dreams of a future with hope in it. I hate alcohol for what it did to Mum and Dad, but I have a friend in it too. Tuck it under my wing as an ally in hard times.

'Shall we take the boat out, lads? What do you reckon?' says Swanny.

Robin and I shrug and then stand up, push the boat into the lake and clamber in. Do what he tells us, like always. The boat steadies itself, and I try not to panic whilst the black water laps up against its empty barrel.

We push out and the last of the light falls from the sky. Soon, everything is grainy like a bad photo. The night wraps around us, pins us down.

A handful of birds fall sideways across the indigo sky. Why so much energy, birds? I wonder. What's in it for you?

I lean up against the prow, wondering how I let myself get into this. Why had we even come up to the lake? Why had I said yes? I rest my head back against my hands, slink down low in the boat. Rob slouches down too, looking back towards me, and Swanny sits behind him, looking out at the water as if he's on Titanic or something.

It is only over this empty, aimless summer, that we've started to hang out. Everyone else seems to have pissed off somewhere, or maybe they can't be arsed to leave their front door, that's the way that it is these days, gaming all day long. It's just us three that have nothing better to do than go joyriding in rowing boats.

'What are you doing after college then Swan?' I call out, the lager sloshing about in my belly. Anything to distract myself from the fact that I'm rocking about in a poxy wooden boat on a lake after several cans of dodgy lager.

'Ain't bothered,' he says.

Always acts like he doesn't give a toss about anything.

'But this is your chance, mate. Get the hell out.'

Swanny shrugs and leans down to drag his hand through the water.

'Same here as anywhere else, isn't it? What's so good about mainland?'

'Well, it's not here, for a start,' says Robin. 'Wish we could still get to Europe. Mum caught a train around when she was eighteen, hopping on and off wherever she liked. Different world then.'

The reality of it hits me again. A tiny stab.

'Can't last forever, can they, these sanctions?' Robin says. 'Shit scary, isn't it?'

We murmur in agreement.

'Have you ever wondered if it's our own government,' Swanny says, 'Like with the Berlin wall — it was their own folks keeping them in, wasn't it?'

The thought had crossed my mind too, but I couldn't really believe it was all a conspiracy. What would be the point of hemming in your own people?

'Doesn't mean we can't dream,' I say. 'Might not be able to go anywhere now, but that doesn't mean we stop thinking about it. Things'll open up sooner or later, they have to.'

'Do they? This could be it.'

My heart starts to race.

I force myself to breathe slowly.

In. Out.

'It'll be okay,' I say to myself. Then out loud, with a nervous laugh, 'Nah, you'll see, you'll see.'

Don't know if I believe it myself, but hope is the only thing dragging me onwards, however fanciful it may be.

These moments of pure panic have been happening more and more. They build up inside me, a mass of spiders crawling on the inside of my brain. Makes me want to burst open with a scream. Feels like there is so much inside of me and I can't get it out.

Meds are getting thin on the ground now, but almost everyone I know is on happy pills. Takes the edge off. That and booze. My pills ran out a few weeks ago and I'm trying to manage without them. Mostly by not thinking about the bigger picture. Head down. Not much choice anyway — pharmacies ain't getting them in. So, folks eke them out. One on a bad day.

'I might stay around here, go out on the boats,' says Swanny. 'Can't take the sea off us, can they? Besides, what's Mam going to do if I scarper?'

'She'll be right, meet another man,' chips in Robin.

Swanny shrugs, frowns.

'She doesn't need another man. I mean, I'm all she's got, know what I mean?'

It's the same with Dad. I can't imagine leaving him on the island.

The water laps up against the boat and I trail my hand in it.

'Either that or wait for the power station to open back up again. Pay's pretty good I hear.'

'That's coz they're all getting nuked just working there,' smirks Robin.

The new mega nuclear power station at Sheerness, that was meant to provide lucrative jobs and feed the UK and half of France with power, had been decommissioned the day they closed the borders. We couldn't afford to run it anymore.

'I might go to mainland, see what's happening up London way, get to the bottom of this,' I say. *Find Mum*, I think.

I'm not naive enough to think that I could change something myself, but maybe I could rally some support or put pressure on the government to find a way out? Maybe I could write about it, get to the heart of the matter? Doing anything has to be better than biding my time on the island. That's why I try to keep my head down and study, even though college is falling down around my feet. It's my only passport out of here. No one else gives a shit anymore.

'We can't be tied down though boys;' I rattle on. 'This is it, time to run free. I fancy journalism, make a difference with my pen, find out what's really going in Europe.'

'Mate, you'll never make a difference.' Swanny laughs. 'This is just the way it is now. How are you going to open the borders with your pen?'

I shrug, murmur, 'Dunno.'

They must wonder who the hell I think I am to be able to get out of here. No one else has managed it. I can though, I know it. Dog with a bone. Won't stop until I'm on mainland.

'And your dad?' asks Robin.

'He'll never leave, he's told me as much.'

The other thing that I really want churns over in my mind because I know I can never have it again: all of us together — Me, Mum, Dad, Zoe.

I remember the steelworks clattering and banging through the night, down on the coast; the town is used to drifting to sleep against its noise. Well, it was. Since the Cut Off, when it closed, we don't hear it anymore, but like a ghost limb, I still feel it — clanking through the night, bringing our mums and dads some livelihood, some sense of pride, however small.

'There's a change coming, has to be.' I say, 'Can feel it.' And I hope with everything in me that I'm right.

But still the thoughts roll over and over in my mind.

Tick, tick, tick go the old anxieties.

'We should be rolling in the glory of being seventeen, of having it all before us, shouldn't we?' I say, spreading my arms open. 'Of finding the big wide world, of finding our purpose,' I say, the overflow of my tipsy thoughts spewing up into the night sky.

'Lager's got you hoping too high, Jay... Let it go.'

Swanny takes a long drag on his cigarette and blows a ring of smoke up to meet my thoughts.

'Whatever you say Jay,' Robin chips in, quietly. 'I hope you're right. I hope there's a bit of the big wide world left for us to find.'

The silence falls between us then and there's just the water again, lapping against the boat, and the far-off hum of life, the quiet ssh of the waves. There is the echo chamber of the island again, turning in on itself as it always has — in defence of the sea, or the outside, or something.

Swanny pulls another four-pack from his rucksack, and says, 'Sod the future lads, let's get merry.'

'Seriously, mate ... how?'

He grins.

I take a can, pop it open and put it down next to me on the bottom of the rowing boat without taking a swig. I let out a sigh and look up at smudgy sky.

I roll over to take a sip of lager. Everything tumbles through me: the black water, the booze sloshing around in my stomach, all the things that Mum couldn't do to save herself. When she drank, the alcohol warmed her from the inside and made her think she could do anything — climb a building, swim to Holland, fall in love again. Oh Mum.

I curl up under the bench at the prow of the boat, my stomach already churning from the three cokes and two lagers I'd had before.

Closing my eyes, I breathe a deep lungful of air, and I see Mum, crystal clear, sitting on the shore. She's wearing her navy anorak, her brown hair falling around her shoulders. Her knees are pulled up to her chest and her arms wrap around them tightly. She flicks her cigarette ash down onto the pebbles, downs the rest of her bottle of cider and stands.

And then she walks into the sea, fully clothed, as if it is just a normal road. She takes everything with her, the bottle, the cigarette, all of her clothes. The whole of her smallness just walks out into the waves. She shivers as the water laps about her thighs, and then just keeps going, calm and languid as the black night, as this black lake. The tip of her cigarette glows as she gets further away.

'No!' I shout, sitting up bolt upright.

The boat rocking on the water has taken its toll on my stomach, and I fall over to one side, moaning, 'I think I'm going to—' and then I interrupt myself by heaving my guts out into the lake. 'Sorry lads,' I say, weakly, between episodes of heaving. 'Think I must be seasick.'

Swanny howls with delight.

'Seasick? We're on a lake, you daft sod! Seasick?'

I groan.

Seasick on a rowing boat on a lake? A fear of water at the age of seventeen, whilst living on an island? The more distorted my life has become the more I see all this baggage that I carry — fear of water, fear of leaving in case Mum comes back, fear of being abandoned.

The more I keep myself to myself, the more normal I feel. It's just when I'm with others that it highlights what a total freak I am.

Rob's cool though. He knows everything, and he doesn't mind.

I fall back and close my eyes, but my thoughts keep

circling in neon. If Mum had cheated on Dad, he'd have forgiven her. I couldn't blame her for wanting to fall in love again. But that wasn't what took her away from him, she cheated on him in her mind. She imagined a new life for herself. One where nothing went wrong, where love always lasted. I didn't blame her for that either, who could? Maybe that's what she was doing. Maybe she went to mainland. Went to find herself. Not the water though.

Next year, I'll find her. I'll make things right again. She can't be dead. She can't be.

The wave of sickness subsides, and I stand up, breathe deeply.

And then a hand jabs hard into my ribs. My body contorts as I try to regain my balance, but it is too late. I let out a shout before my body crashes against the surface of the lake with a slap.

I take in a mouthful of water and imagine whitened, bloated bodies beneath me. I sink beneath the surface again and the lake's black skin sweeps over me.

I splash my way to the surface, screaming, 'I can't swim!'

A mouthful of water.

I gasp a lungful of air, fighting and splashing at the water around me.

'I can't swim!' I shout, before going under again. 'Swanny!' I shout, smacking the surface of the water with the flats of my hands.

'Here, grab on!' he shouts, pushing an oar under the water. 'Jay! Jay?'

I can hear his faraway voice and I reach out to grab hold of the oar.

Robin tries to haul me into the boat, but I am a dead weight in the water. I cling on to the side of the boat, my teeth chattering.

'Give us a hand then!' he shouts to Swanny.

Swanny snaps out of his reverie and hauls me over the side. I roll over, coughing and spluttering.

Swanny stands in the rowing boat, his arms folded over his chest, an idiotic smile upon his face, gazing out into the night.

'I'll give you seasick,' he murmurs.

'He can't swim! Fuck's got into you?' Rob shouts.

Swanny stands there, looking straight ahead. Smirks.

'You should have said,' he finally comes out with, in a strange, calm voice.

'I didn't know you were going to push me in the sodding lake!' I screech, between snatched breaths.

A half-smile on his lips.

'You should really learn to swim,' he says. 'You live on an island.'

I feel like I could start sobbing any minute, so I concentrate on my breathing.

'There's a bridge, ain't there?' I shrug, laughing. But I can't pretend. I am as see-through as a greenhouse, no tricks up my sleeve, no superpowers. A thin bravado made thicker by beer, that's all. I am a coward, a let-down. A freak.

He has it in his grasp now, my Achille's heel. Water. I dread to think what he'll do next.

Swanny keeps us at arm's length, never talks about himself. Noticed that.

'Didn't you learn to swim at school like, Jay?' asks Rob, frowning. 'We did life savers in Year 8, didn't we?'

'Nah, mate, never been a strong swimmer.'

I shiver as I try to catch my breath.

'I swear we did it with Mr Roberts!'

'Haven't swam in years. Weak heart. Row back to the shore, man, I'll get on home now.'

Rob frowns. He takes the oars and begins to swing the boat around and head back to the shore. I watch his face change. The things he knows; what had happened to Mum ... all that Swanny doesn't know. I can imagine his thought trail: He used to swim. He got his lifesavers award. But after what happened with his mum, he couldn't get back in the water.

Missing. Presumed drowned.

Rob gives me a nod, which means, *I get it, I won't say anything.* Why give Swanny any more ammo than he already has?

The only sound then is the water slapping against the side of the boat, Rob's breath as he exerts himself, and my heaving chest, as I gather my own breath.

A steely silence from Swanny as he looks out the other way.

2

JAY

F riday 24th September 2021

AND THEN THERE is a noise coming.
A feathered flapping.

ROB STOPS ROWING to look up.

IT IS COMING CLOSER.

IN THE BLUE grey of dusk,
they are coming,

.   .   .

A MASS OF THEM, darting and looping,
  filling up the whole sky

AND THEY ARE STILL COMING,
  more, and more, and more of them.

THE SKY TURNS black with thousands of feathered bodies.

THEY FLY AS ONE BODY,
  twisting and turning in the painted sky,

THEY MAKE shapes with their one-ness,
  a moon, a cloud, an arm, a shield.

THE RUSTLE of their wings is shingle thrown against a sea
floor,
  it is the mass of water tumbling over a waterfall,
  it is the approach of a high-speed train.

IT IS WEIGHT, power, thrust.
  All of them working as one,
  a multitudinous body.

THEY ARE a cloak of darkness over the lake,
  turning over and over in the silvery light.

· · ·

Their calls are like a chorus of crows.

They fly to the horizon and back again,
    as if they are being shaken in a cage.

They are a black and beautiful swarm,
    shaken out upon the crumpled tablecloth of the island.

They break and remake their body,
    rolling over, reforming, rejoining.

Then they come back and stay, dancing over the lake,
    overhead, for half an hour, maybe more.

Then, in a breath, their blackness dissipates
    and the bird-cloud pales as it dances away to the north
of the island.

We watch silently. Swanny stands up to see it go. And
then, afterwards a feeling like the peace that comes over you
when you are all cried out.
    'Woah,' Swanny whispers.
    'That was unreal,' I murmur.
    'Freaky,' says Rob.

· · ·

EVERYTHING THAT HAPPENED BEFORE IS FORGOTTEN. SURPASSED by this.

It doesn't seem right to talk about it, so we let it rest between us.

I SHIVER in my wet clothes and roll over into a foetal position for Rob's last few strokes to shore. I feel unnerved. As if someone is watching me. It isn't just the vision of Mum — this lake has always freaked me out. I've heard tales of children whose cries didn't resurface here. Talk of an old boy who waded in with stones in his pockets after he lost his wife. Couldn't go on without her. I would never come up here on my own. There were ghosts, and too many stories.

It's the thought of Mum, floating unfound for all these years. That's why I stopped swimming after she went, I couldn't face it. Anyway. She has to be alive; she pulls me onwards.

I'm terrified the water will call me too, so I edge around it. An untameable terror, lurking in the background of each day. Framing my life with its power and the unshakeable feeling that I am surrounded.

But the birds.

How majestic, how beautiful, how silencing is their presence.

IT FEELS as if they were trying to communicate to us, to tell us something. They had our undivided attention; we were utterly captivated. But what had they come to say?

'They're the only ones who are still free, aren't they?' I say. 'They can go wherever they like.'

Swanny looks down at the inky water, trails his hand in it.

'Sorry for earlier, mate,' he says, without looking up. 'I don't know what came over me.'

But even the way he says it gives me the chills.

I don't look at him as we pull the boat back up on to a patch of shingle, hear the crunch of it on the underbelly of the boat, lash it to the stake, go our separate ways. I can hear Swanny and Rob's wittering fade as they wander back into town.

Rob is wary of him too, I can tell.

I take the other path, up over the grass verge and along the railway tracks back to the caravan park. There's a full moon — it lights up the tracks a little way before me and I suddenly have an urge to run as fast as I can, to fill my lungs with the cool air. I sprint along the track and let out a yelp of something – joy, fear, exhilaration ... something between them all. Sometimes I have this urge to get to the end of myself, to exhaust myself with speed — the pace and graft of it. There isn't enough spending myself, otherwise. Not enough living, in these empty days.

As I near the lane that runs down to the caravan park, my t-shirt gets caught on a bramble, which scratches across my body and curls around my leg. I can't stop though. I'm going too fast, and the momentum carries me, even as the bramble scores through my skin. I shout out and keep on running, and my shout is covered up by the rush of the night train sailing past me on the tracks.

I stumble back to the caravan and change out of my damp clothes, my teeth chattering as I balance on one leg to try to pull my wet jeans off, full of lake water.

My alarm clock reads 23.47.

I crawl into bed naked, pull the sheets up close to my chin, and fall asleep, shivering, dreaming of black water, of Mum.

3

JAY

Saturday 25th September 2021

THE SUN POURS through the orange curtains, and my tongue is a hot slug in my mouth.

'I need a drink,' I say out loud, to no one.

I put my hand up to my cheek, to a crusted line of something on my face. It smarts to the touch, and I groan, remembering the brambles.

I sit up too quickly, and realise I still feel sick from the beer, the anxiety of being on the lake, the black water that I swallowed. I shudder at the thought of the beer and lake water mixing around in my gut.

I pull on some joggers and stumble through to the kitchen, stepping on the sodden mound of clothes on my bedroom floor that I'd stripped off the night before. I pour myself a glass of water and sip a little to calm my stomach. The washing up hasn't been done. No surprises there.

It's 7.30. Dad's normally up by now, making his breakfast, heading out of the door by 8. If he's got any work that is.

'Dad?' I call. 'You got any work today? You'll be late!'

No reply.

'Dad!' I call, a little louder. 'Do you want a cuppa?'

I push open the door to his room. He isn't there.

The sheets are puckered, wrinkled, look slept in. Odd. I hadn't thought to check last night. I just went straight to sleep.

Maybe he went out walking, I think. *Maybe he's gone to work early.*

Neither option is likely.

There is a knock at the door. An urgent knock. Like something is wrong.

Robin is standing there, clutching the hand of his little sister Ava. His cheeks are red, but his face is pale at the same time. Breathlessly, he starts to talk.

'They're gone,' he says. 'They're all gone. Your Dad?'

I look at him, blankly.

I shake my head. 'Dad's not here. Wondered if he'd stepped out—'

Robin cuts me off mid-sentence, shaking his head. 'They're *all* gone.'

His chest is heaving. He's obviously ran all the way from his, with Ava.

Goosebumps prickle along my arms.

'My mum,' Robin says, between breaths. 'Ava wandered into her room this morning like she always does, gets in bed for a cuddle. But the bed was cold, her t-shirt and leggings laid out like she'd been in it, in the shape of how she lay. Ava screamed and I woke up and came in. We looked for her, any sign of her leaving. Tried to remember the last thing I said to her, but we'd gone out, hadn't we? I hadn't stopped for dinner, I just went down the chippie. Her bag's there though, her phone is charging. Her keys are there, the car's there.'

He looks at me.

Ava looks down and sways, sniffing the tears back.

'I just don't understand it.'

'Mate, calm down. I'm sure there's an explanation,' I say, beckoning them in. 'Maybe she just went to the shop?'

Robin barges past me and into Dad's room.

'Jay, aren't you listening to me? They've gone. Look ...' Robin points to the bed. 'Your dad's pyjamas are laid out like he was still asleep in them, just like Mum's were. Let me a get a photo,' he says, and pulls out his phone to capture it.

'I've tried ringing 999,' he carries on, at a hundred miles an hour, 'but the mobile network is down. A message is playing that I've never heard before. It says: "The network you are trying to activate does not exist".'

'What the hell? The network does not exist?'

'I know!'

'What's going on Robin?' I say, feeling like I'm being particularly dense, feeling like I haven't woken up properly and nothing is making sense.

'I don't know what's going on, mate,' Robin's lip wobbles as if he is going to crumble.

I put a hand on his arm. 'It's ok. We'll work it out.' I try to be calm for Ava, who's only four, and rub my eyes, trying to get my brain to wake up. 'So, your mum and my dad have both disappeared? What are you saying, that they're having an affair?'

Robin shakes his head in exasperation. 'Look out of the window, Jay.'

I lift the net curtain. Children are milling about in their

pyjamas, holding hands, crying. For a few seconds I can't figure it out. And then I realise.

'The adults,' Robin says. 'They've gone. All of them.'

I stare at him. 'What?'

My heart races in my chest.

'What do you mean?' I laugh, and then see his face, his hollow eyes. 'But that's impossible.'

'We went out to the green and all these kids started to emerge from their houses, looking for someone responsible, someone to help them. We let them into our house, and now we're gathering everyone we can find. We need your help, Jay. We need to find them all. I don't know what to do.'

I stand there in a daze. All I have is questions, but my brain won't put them into words. I put on my hoodie, slip my useless phone into my back pocket, and follow Robin and Ava outside.

'And there's another thing,' Robin says. 'The birds. There are dead birds all over the place.'

4

JAY

W ednesday 4th August 2021

TWO MONTHS EARLIER

'WHAT ARE WE GONNA DO, DAD?' I say. He's just picked up a chippy lunch. Literally just chips. We're not allowed to fish our own waters anymore.

'You what?'

'I mean, is this it? Benefits and chips?'

He shrugs.

'I think I was cut out for more. No offence.'

'You're soft in the head, son. There ain't nothing round here.'

'So, let's go! Cannery's been closed six months now. When I leave for uni next year, come with me! I'll get in somewhere; we'll find a flat on the mainland. You can find a job doing something different. London? South Coast? Chance for a fresh start.'

Dad doesn't acknowledge me, just stares at the TV screen and picks at his food, shoving limp chips into his mouth while I stand awkwardly to one side. There is a re-run of *Countdown* on TV. It's all re-runs these days. He pretends not to hear me.

Giving up on life here means he will have to admit that his life is shit, which it invariably is.

'Ah, I almost had that. *Knowledge*. Tricky one.' He sucks in his breath and takes a swig of his home brew. Tastes like piss.

'Haven't you got any more work this week then?'

'Bits and bobs, day here or there, they said. Nothing regular like.'

He's signed on with an agency up in Sheerness for manual labour since he'd lost the cannery job. He's had a few days' work, fixing fences up on Garret farm, hauling sacks about. Manual stuff. After the Cut Off, everyone went back to the land.

'Something will come along, Dad; you're only young.'

'Pah!' He spits violently, wiping the grease from his mouth with the back of his hand. 'Young, he says! What does it matter these days if we're young or not?'

Trade has fallen off a cliff. The power plant closed. The cannery couldn't shift their tins of fish and went bust overnight, which meant that Dad had no work. When he lost his job, we couldn't afford the rent on the flat, and then we ended up here on the caravan park at Leysdown. We didn't need a three bed anymore, what with Mum and Zozo and the council had run out of other options. Life is a stack of dominoes and when one goes, they all do.

I don't mind it here so much, though. The caravans all

face inwards, towards a green. It's like we've got our backs to the world and it's nice, kind of. Feels like we're one big family. Everyone looks out for each other. The little kids mess about on the grass, so their folks can see them, and the older kids race their bikes around the back. The storms wrap and whirl over the top, rattling the caravans on their paving slabs.

It's so dark at night; feels like we're perched on the edge of the world.

And even though it's a come-down, it's our own place. And even though Mum won't know where to find us, if she ever comes back, we aren't far away.

Living in a caravan through winter is something else; and we only got the dregs of it. In March, when we moved in, my face would hurt with the cold in the mornings. We wore jumpers and coats inside, could see our breath whirling out of our mouths as we ate breakfast. I used to sleep in a jumper, used to have to psyche myself up for a shower. The power would go out if you boiled the kettle and switched the heater on at the same time.

Aside from winter, though, it's not so bad.

Load of families came down here after the Cut Off. The shame got turned to attitude; we didn't know what else to do with it.

Now there's a whole bunch of us waiting for something to change, for some work to come in, someone to get rich, someone to win the lottery. It's like that around here. You're waiting for the change but aren't quite brave enough to make it happen.

So, you just hang around and wait to see what life brings your way, flotsam and jetsam, like.

Us islanders ain't world changers. Stuff just seems to happen to us.

Up in London, they make all these decisions and we bear the brunt of it. But their games didn't work out either, and the door has been slammed on them too. I could say I told you so but we're all in it together so what's the point?

It was New Year's Day when they said the borders were closing. Seven months ago, and I remember it as clear as yesterday. The PM had just announced the beginning of the UK's glorious transition out of the European Free Republic, and then the news flicked to a live press conference with the leader of the EFR. She looked straight at the camera (down the barrel of the gun), her eyes like fire, and said:

'Today, January 1ˢᵗ, the UK has been irrevocably ejected from the EFR and placed under sanctions for tax evasion and fraud during its membership. For the foreseeable future, there will be no passage in or out of the UK. All trade will cease between the UK and the rest of the world. Your borders are closed with immediate effect.'

We were in the Black Dog, as usual, watching it on the TV.

'Ere, what did she just say?' piped up one of the old boys. He wore a tired looking suit and propped up the bar.

'Dunno mate,' answered someone else. 'Does it bother us though? We're free of the EFR now, aren't we?'

'Irrevocably ejected?' Old Pete repeated slowly. 'That don't sound good.'

He looked up to the ceiling whilst wiping a glass with a tea towel.

Then the ribbon appeared, passing across the bottom of the news broadcast: 'UK FORCIBLY EJECTED FROM THE EFR.'

'But we're leaving anyway, aren't we?' said Kenny, shaking his head, a look of confusion over his face. He ran the amusements down at the front in summer, hung around with nothing to do all winter. 'What's all the fuss about?'

A ripple of unease passed through the room. The news kept rolling all night. We wandered home, wondering what it all meant, assuming the PM knew how to fix it.

We got back to the flat and made tea to warm our hands on as we watched the news. The news fed us the party line, but it was on Twitter that the shock of the nation unfolded. #cutoff was trending, and that was how it felt.

'Well, that's some happy new year,' Dad murmured, as he fell into a doze, holding his empty *Wispa* mug on his chest.

'Come on Dad. It'll come right in the morning,' I said, nudging him, and taking the mug from his hands before he spilled lukewarm tea down his chest. He stumbled off to bed, while I sat there, refreshing my Twitter feed over and over, waiting for the news to be different, waiting for it all to be a mistake.

If there's one thing Mum left me with, it was the sense to trust my gut, and right then a deep sense of unease was making its home inside me. It twisted down in me as I watched the news. There's a lot Mum left me with. Questions, mostly.

You could see the shock on the faces of the news readers, even though they were supposed to be impartial. You could see it in the PM's face as he was shuffled onto the stage the next day to make an emergency statement. No one had seen it coming. He tried to make light of it, rocking back on his heels, saying, 'It's just talks, no need to panic. We will have this resolved by the end of the week.' But his bloodshot eyes and thrown-on suit gave away the fact that it had knocked him for six, too.

It took a few weeks for the shock to wear away from the

news readers' faces. There was talk of the Confederacy of Nations or the US coming to help us, but when it came down to it, they all turned away. The agreement was signed and they couldn't get out of it even if they wanted to. It was already in motion. For a month, at least, the talk was: 'Is this legal?', 'Can they do this?', and the consensus was yes, actually. The UK had broken the terms of its contract agreement, and the EFR reserved the right to impose sanctions, providing they were agreed by the CoN. And when the CoN was basically run by the EFR, there was no hope.

'No passage,' they said, like madmen, and it stuck.

And so, we found ourselves cut off by the cold North Sea. An island nation all to ourselves. We didn't know why the EFR were herding us into a corner. There was something behind it, there had to be. The sanctions seemed so far out of proportion to whatever we were supposed to have done. It made us wonder if there was a step two in their plans. And then we felt strangely vulnerable.

AFTER THE CUT OFF, the sense of being hemmed in made you feel like your brains were slowly boiling in your skull. You had to remind yourself to breathe. You had to stand looking at the sea for long stretches of time, just to calm yourself down. You had to take one day at a time, because if you looked to your future, it would run away from you laughing.

I remember thinking, if only we could be like birds we could fly up and settle somewhere new. But it seemed pretty settled now. This was the way it was going to be. Nothing had changed in nine months. Things had just got steadily worse.

.   .   .

AT THE BEGINNING, the government said they were doing everything they could to get medicines manufactured in the UK, that there was no need to stockpile, so of course, everyone stockpiled which made things worse. Dad's Mum, Lily, couldn't get what she needed. She was in constant pain with arthritis, could barely move her knees. We kept begging the pharmacy for her meds, but they would just shrug their shoulders.

Every time I had to explain to Gran, her face fell.

I thought about trying to get her some on the black market, just to make things a bit easier, but you never really knew what you were buying, and it cost a fortune. In the end, she learned to live with the pain.

Just this week, the government said everyone should have their essential medication by Friday, but no one can get what they need.

Folks are angry. Food is thinning out. Things cost twice what they used to. And the benefits aren't going up.

So, we eke things out, eat less, keep ourselves to ourselves. It's surprising how quickly a country can fall apart. Two days ago, the government got on their hands and knees and said they needed help.

Some days the fear could eat me alive, but against all this, life still goes on.

School, eating, walking, the pub.

But the idea of the future is getting more and more hazy. Almost as if our island has become shrouded in fog. We can't see clearly, aren't sure which way to go.

I'm clinging on to the fact that I will get off the island next year for Uni. I just have to bide my time until then.

I won't torment Dad anymore, he clearly doesn't want to talk about it, so I give up. He's a brick wall sometimes. I know he loves me, but he's pretty hard to communicate with.

I pick up the plate by his feet and the two mugs from the windowsill that have cold, grey tea floating around in the bottom of them. I take them over to the sink where I try to wash up silently, so Dad can watch *Countdown* in peace.

It's ok to want more isn't it? I think.

I stack the washing-up neatly and go to sit on the metal step outside the door. I take a rationed ciggy from my pocket and light it.

I have to be good, I think. *I have to be responsible.*

I hold Dad up, I am cheerful, I am hopeful. If I am not good, then I will probably fall apart.

I have to keep it together. I don't have a choice.

It doesn't feel like Dad is in this with me; he's on his own little island, out at sea. I guess it's his way of coping. I'm not angry with him; I'd forgive him anything. He doesn't seem to try, though. He just gets through the day. We talk about the state of the country, but only in vague terms that we hear on the news. It's not our tongue; it doesn't fit us to talk politics. It doesn't fit us to be eco-warriors either, but that's the way things are going.

'Dad,' I say, leaning back through the caravan door. 'Do you think we should be growing our own veg?'

'Yeah, we could give it a crack son,' he shouts back. 'If you like.'

Wonder if we can grow anything this year. Probably left it too late. A project with Dad, something to drag him away from the gameshows. A little bit of time together before the summer wanes, the heat falls out of the days, and the darkness comes around again.

November is when Mum went, and I crawl slowly through the month each year.

This year, of all the years, I don't quite know how we'll get through. And when I say we, I mean us, but also the whole country, this new world.

Sometimes, you think all this effort, all this living, what is it really for?

And sometimes I wonder why I am so desperate to get to next summer. What will I do then? But a quiet voice inside my head reminds me. *Leave. That's what you'll do. That's what you've been waiting for all along.*

I realise I am done waiting for something to change. I want...no, I *have* to be the change this time, even if that means leaving Dad.

5
———

JAY

S unday 8th August 2021

I'VE TAKEN TO WALKING. It gets me away from Dad, gets me the space I need. I go early, before he wakes. I've already been out as far as the prison, but I know if I push a little further and cut across the farming land, I'll be out in the marshland. I've felt the pull of it for days. I need to be out there on my own with the birds and the water.

I live in my head a lot these days. It feels as if my life is a Rubik's cube that I have to figure out. What does the future hold, how can I get Dad to take me seriously? When is the hope coming, the tide turning?

I walk down towards New Rides farm, past the hulking mass of the prisons on my right. The path leads down a narrow grass track, and then there is a gate and freedom beyond.

A gravel track leads through the vast and open marsh.

There is a vista of birds, and the pink sun up in the east. The fog still hangs low over the wet grass, and it lifts as the warmth of the day settles in.

There is a house planted there, inexplicably. Three storeys high, in the middle of the marshland. The path runs right by it, and I can see the house is well looked after, with its neat wall and careful flowers, a watering can by the back door, and a washing line strung from the porch to the west wall.

What a place to live, I think, *out here in the wild all the time. Living with this unstoppable wind in your ears.*

As I pass, I look in. A figure moves about inside, shuffling around with the rhythms of the morning. Tea. Bread. It feels so personal, the daily routine, and so intimate; the comfort found in the smallest of things. A cup of tea made just right, toast the way you like it, not too much butter, not too much jam.

I am intruding on a private moment, a moment of personal readying for the day. I walk quickly past.

I have never been somewhere quite so exposed. I'm an outsider here, and vulnerable with it. There is nowhere to hide. I pull my hoodie up over my head and carry on. I am here, no apologies.

I follow the track as it snakes around the reserve, the long six miles of it, all the way up to the farmhouse and back, and it feels that my body is learning to breathe again.

Birds call around me in the damp, pink morning, and everything feels kind of new. The dew has made crystals on the blades of grass. As I walk, a flock of white birds leap into the sky in a breath. They swirl and squawk around me while they weigh up whether I am a threat. Having decided I am not, they float down again, light as feathers, to their roosting places.

A whole sky of them awake gives me a burn in the pit of myself.

'It's time to take flight,' I whisper.

Hemmed in? Look at this place. All the sky is awake, the whole world is awake and here I am, breathing it all in.

'How can I be trapped with all this at my heel?' I whisper to myself.

6

ELSIE

Sunday 8th August 2021

ELSIE GRAYLING PEERS out of her shutters at the grey sky looming like a bad thought.

'Storm coming,' she says, matter-of-factly, as she clears away her lunch plate, clatters her plate and mug into the small ceramic sink and runs the hot tap.

The boiler fires into life. She scrubs the plate and mug with a scouring pad and puts them in the plastic rack to drip dry, then boils the kettle for a coffee. Marmite on toast is all she needs some days. Hot tea and coffee, too, all day long. Warms her in the winter, occupies her in the summer.

She is well used to talking to herself. There's the dog, Bernie, though, who potters around her feet. He listens, kind of, but she doesn't mind if he falls asleep. She'd talk to the walls if he wasn't there. Some days she's too deep in thought to talk, even to herself. On days like those the sound of her own voice shocks her into being.

She's already been out on her rounds today. She goes as early as she can, walks six or seven miles a day, which takes her four hours or thereabouts and she's back in time for lunch. Afternoons are for writing. Surveys. If not surveys then articles. If not articles then poems, and if not poems, then pen and ink drawings, with Bernie napping across her feet like a hot water bottle. Evenings are for reading.

And that is it, the sum of her life, mapped out into little boxes. The rest of the time is spent on the mundane. Laundry, house repairs, getting supplies.

Since her student days, when she first visited the island, it had plumbed the depths of her. She hadn't intended to stay, but it called to her, and she couldn't say no.

She studied conservation at UEA and saw an article all about the wild and desolate island. It said that the RSPB were going to take over the marshes, and they were calling for volunteers. She'd never been before, but it intrigued her, this wilderness, right in the crook of the Thames estuary. A hidden treasure.

Her friends at university had called it bleak, when Elsie said where she was going, but she was unperturbed and signed up for an apprenticeship the following year.

That same year the place had got under her skin – the way the fog danced over the marsh in the morning, the way the birds trusted the reserve, the big, empty skies with the skinny, white clouds drawn across them. It was everything she wanted.

She loves living out on the limb of the estuary. Her house is a flag in the wind, and she is the watchkeeper. Over the years, the farms had merged, the cement works closed, and the marsh had emptied out. Nothing there, was there? Nothing worth staying for. Used to be on its own isle, this reserve, but the cut that divided it from the rest of the isle silted up over time. The workers all went, and then it was just the sheep and the birds who had the run of the place.

She still works as a warden for the RSPB on the island, tracking and monitoring the bird populations. The only place she has ever lived where the birds have dominion, the only place where she feels peace in her soul.

Sure, life is shot to bits with the Cut Off, but all she has ever wanted is this life. What does it matter that they are cast adrift in the North Sea when they have these skies, these birds?

The RSPB pay her a stipend to be guardian of the meres now. Minister to the birds. A measly sum, but the house comes with it so she can't complain. Just as the RSPB were turning the whole place into a bird reserve, she said: 'I'll mind the cottage, just until things are better.' She knew then that she'd never leave.

Later, when the RSPB wanted to hand ownership of the property back to the private owners, she asked for a clause to be added so she couldn't be evicted until she died. After she was gone, she didn't care what they did. They could bulldoze the house for all she cared. By then she'd be with the birds anyway. The RSPB need her work, they've told her as much, and in return, she watches. Tells them what she sees and what is amiss. Walks the marshes every day and notices. Has done for thirty years.

Strange encyclopaedia, she has in her mind now.

She doesn't see folk much these days, just the landowners, who come by every now and then. Nods her head to them on the lanes. Walks with a stick, as tall as her shoulder. It has gained her the nickname of Strange Shepherdess. The islanders are suspicious of her, which she doesn't mind. It keeps them away, which she is quietly grateful for.

They know her old house, the cold, single-paned house, out on the marshlands – one room thick and three storeys high. Windows on both sides, sea and sky all around her. She feels part of the estuary here, and she lives in its changing air. In summer, she can smell the salt before she gets out of bed. In winter, there is ice on the inside of the windowpanes.

The bones of the old house rattle in winter, when the wind from the estuary rushes under the front door. The walls are too thin. The Swale rushes along, whirling and swirling, and she lives in the eye of it all.

There is no central heating, just a wood burner in the sitting room, so in winter Elsie wears as many layers as she can – a thermal vest, two thick wool jumpers, a gilet, and a scarf. Under her bulk of clothes, she is skeletal, bird-like.

She is aware that she lives like a raving old thing on the reserve, but she likes it that way. The sparse life keeps her ready, like a sharpened pencil, for whatever is coming.

She has made her life quiet so she can marvel each day at these birds. The soaring might of a thousand tiny things. Bernie doesn't mind, he's her constant companion, keeping her from going completely mad.

'So much to do,' she mutters as she goes about her chores. Some days there seems a lifetime of work ahead of her still, and yet some days she thinks she is nearing the end. She still submits to the journals that will take her work, but she has encountered snobbery too. She hadn't gone as far as the others, hadn't been to the best schools, wasn't called up to run seminars in conservation. But if you were talking about the heart of it, she still had it. If you were going by the love, she was still the queen.

The things she knows about her birds are by sight, by heart. She can tell if something is bothering them, if something is out of balance, but she doesn't have the letters after her name to prove it.

No one comes to the house anymore, they haven't for years; she doesn't have the patience for it. No time for tittle-tattle, she has a job to do.

But something had changed out on the marsh that day.

There was a boy out there this morning, hesitant but wandering. He had nowhere to go, she could tell. Not like herself and the twitchers, who marched the long tracks with impatience, he was ambling, unsure, watching.

She wondered what he was looking for.

7

SUANZIE

M onday 9th August 2021

WHAT THE HELL have I come to? Suzie wonders some days. *Why am I still here, in this arse end of nowhere?*

She's sure there's somewhere else for her to go, she just isn't sure where. And when you want to take flight, surely you must know where you want to go.

She sure as hell hadn't imagined running a sweetshop on the island, in her forties.

'It's only a job,' she whispers. 'Deep breath.' As the door-bell pings, a woman lugging a pushchair, backs awkwardly into the shop.

Oh well, maybe it didn't matter if her life had come to nothing. *They're all in the shit now, aren't they?* she thinks, smugly. It gives her a sick kind of comfort, that even Trish, the friend who made it, couldn't just jet off to St Lucia now, could she? The flights are all grounded. The planes just sit there. The cabin crew turn up at work, to welcome no one, because the planes aren't allowed to fly. They're all in limbo, waiting for something to change.

Suzie has to laugh at it all. If she doesn't laugh, she will cry. And laughing is her very last defence against this government.

Most nights, Suzie can't sleep. Everything falls deathly silent without the drone of planes going off to Europe and America. She feels completely alone, rocked to sleep in the rowing boat of Sheppey, out on its own in the lonely sea.

For the last few weeks, Suzie has been getting dreams of being strangled by a black, shadowy figure, his hands gripping tighter and tighter around her throat, squeezing the air, closing down her airways. She knows what it means, it isn't rocket science. It's how it feels to live these days. She wonders if she needs to do something about it, and how she can stop it from coming back. Is there such a thing as a dream counsellor? She couldn't afford it if there was.

But anxiety, if that's what it is, serves a purpose, doesn't it? Keeps you on edge. Fight or flight. Except there's no one to fight, and nowhere to go. Bit like those planes, just sitting there.

Suzie watches the woman make her way around the edge of the shop, picking up things and setting them down again.

Suzie's phone pings. It's her mum, Lily.

Suz, can you see if they've anything for me at the pharmacy?

Suzie rolls her eyes and taps back.

I'll try Mum, but you know it'll be the same old story

Lily lives close to the edge, out at Shellness. Just her and a few ramshackle houses out on the spit, staring out to sea, like a row of cabins on an ocean liner. There, she walks along the shore, collects driftwood, plays cards and drinks rum with her friends...well, when they could get hold of it. Down to home-brew now. For the most part, they could forget about the real world. Age is biting at her heels though. Sometimes she wakes in the morning and has to wait an hour before she can get out of bed because the pain is so bad. Her body is packing up, but she isn't ready.

She always wanted to live off-grid, in an out-of-the-way sort of a place, and she managed it for years, cycling up to the farm shop every few days for food, but a month ago, she fell and was too scared to get back on the bike again. So now she's stranded. She can't manage with shopping, laundry and all the rest of it and can't bear to depend on her friends, so it's Suzie that she calls on more and more.

Suzie has never liked the house, out there. It feels too close to the ground somehow, as if it will sink or float out to sea. After the last time she fell, it became obvious to Suzie that living out at Shellness wouldn't work anymore. She knew it was time to bring Lily back to live in her flat in Leysdown. She just hadn't got around to telling Lily yet.

The doorbell pings again, and it's Jay, her nephew.

'Hi love! Don't see you in here very often,' she says.

Beautiful boy. All spotty with youth, but with deep, soulful eyes, and brown hair that falls over them. He has a wise head on his shoulders; has to with all he's been through.

'Just walking past. Thought I'd see if you had any freebies,' he says with a cheesy grin.

Suzie rolls her eyes.

'Might have known. What do you fancy?'

'*Snickers*'ll do.'

'Go on then,' she says, and he takes one from the display

under the counter, unwrapping it and taking a bite straight away.

'Stopping production of those, did you hear? Make sure you enjoy it. How are you doing, love?' she asks, but he gestures to his full mouth and gives her a thumbs-up.

'Thanks Aunty Suz. I'll see you around.' He raises the *Snickers* to her as if to toast her kindness.

He disappears out of the door, leaving it to fall shut behind him.

'Bye, love,' she calls out, sadly.

She hasn't seen him for weeks. Still, his mates are probably waiting outside, and she doesn't want to keep him. If only she'd been able to do more for him, to be there for him, somehow, what with everything. Poor Shell.

But she didn't know anything about parenting, so she let him go. Figured that even her dopey brother Jim, would know what he needed more than she did. And now Jay is seventeen, and she can't believe it. All that weight on his skinny shoulders.

She can't imagine having kids of her own now. She thinks back to Trish again, who turned her nose up at the island, the people, the prisons, the shifting light. They'd been the best of friends once. But nothing had been off-limits to her, and she'd kissed Jonathan, the love of Suzie's life, and broken Suzie in the process. Much as she tries to keep her out, Trish creeps into her thoughts most days. She finds herself wondering if they'd still be together now, her and Jonathan. Stupid, really. It was only young love. Her only love.

The woman with the toddler pays for some lollies and tries to back out of the door awkwardly with the pushchair.

'Oh, let me get that for you,' Suzie says, snapping out of her reverie, rushing out from behind the counter to grab the door. Her kindness to strangers is the thing that she wears to hide her loneliness. *Does the woman sense that*, Suzie wonders? Is she overdoing it?

'Have a good day!' she calls out, watching the mother walk off down towards the sea. She doesn't look back.

Suzie longs for September; the final gift of summer with its empty beaches, and mellow mornings. She always shuts up shop at the end of September, so it's all the good things to her: the promise of freedom, the warm, quiet sun. Every year though, the novelty of time off quickly subsides, and she is greeted with the reality of six long, dark months of winter and one month of spring before she opens up again in May.

'What will the world be like then?' she mumbles to herself, brushing sugar crumbs from the countertop. It felt like the whole world was perched at the top of a precipice, about to tip over the edge.

Suzie rings the pharmacy for her mum. Still nothing. She texts Jim, her brother.

We need to talk about Mum

He texts back **K**

She shuts the shop up at five and walks straight up to her mum's to help her cook dinner. The sea is wild out there, and as she walks along the coast path, the light bounces off the sea so brightly it makes her eyes ache.

She fakes brightness for her mum as she gets to the door.

'Hi Mum!'

Lily is sitting on her white sofa, staring out to sea. She is trying to draw it in oil pastels.

'It won't be captured today,' she says with a sigh. 'It won't let me.'

Lily balls up the latest sketch and throws it at the window.

'Mum, the art is supposed to make you feel relaxed, not stress you out!'

Lily shrugs, her face set, staring away.

'It's all running away from me, Suz. Everything I used to be able to do. Who am I if I am no longer me?'

Suzie doesn't know the answer to this, but sits down next to her, holds her hand, and reaches around to give her a hug.

'Oh Mum,' she says. 'You're still you.' And then after waiting a few minutes, 'Let me make you a cup of tea.'

Tea is always the answer.

As Lily sips the tea, she begins to soften, and the words come.

'There was a sand piper out there for twenty minutes today, right outside the door. I went out on the deck, and he hopped away.'

'Oh lovely. Did you get out for a walk then?'

Lily shakes her head, sadly.

'The sea is wild today. I'm not sure I have it in me to swim anymore.'

'Nobody wants to slow down, do they?'

Lily shakes her head again.

Their conversations are getting more and more disjointed, it seems. More and more inane. Lily's Alzheimer's is picking up the pace as well as her arthritis. She doesn't stand a chance against age, this marching machine.

Suzie hates the sound of her own voice sometimes when she's talking to her mother. She knows her words are trite, untrue even, but it's her job to cheer up her mum, so she just makes stuff up. Her mum must be able to tell; she's not stupid.

Suzie puts some rice on to boil and empties chilli from a can into a pan, which she sets on the hob until it bubbles.

Once her mum is happily eating, Suzie washes up and afterwards, helps her into her pyjamas.

'I'll head off now. Have you got everything you need?'

Lily nods.

Suzie feels a pang of guilt as she shuts the door and walks the twenty minutes back along the coast to her flat. She knows she doesn't spend enough time with her, that she just rushes through the jobs and leaves, but it's so boring. Is it ok to say that?

It feels good to be on her own again. True, she is lonely, but she is also unneeded, and she relishes that for a second.

Suzie breathes into the depths of her lungs as the sun blazes its glory over the sea, and the sea crashes upon the quiet shore.

Some things are still good, despite everything.

8

———

JAY

T uesday 10th August 2021

I'VE LEFT IT A DAY, but the marsh calls me again.

I make my excuses to the lads and cycle back to the prisons. I find the footpath that runs between them and down to the wide open.

I leave my bike by the gate and walk out along the pathway, feeling so small. Feeling like this whole wide world is bigger than all of my problems. Bigger even than the Cut Off.

I see a figure, far in the distance, out on the sea wall. They're slightly hunched over, carrying a stick. A little dog runs in front.

A flock of white birds take flight all at once, their backs lit by the sun. They are a shock of beauty. The sun is low and makes golden reflections in the water.

I start walking.

9

SUZIE

ugust 2021

SUZIE KNOCKS on the caravan door.

'Only me!' she calls, through the frosted glass. Jim grunts as he comes to the door in his dressing gown. 'Hiya!'

'What's up with Mum then? Her meds is it?' he says, in a gruff, morning voice.

Suzie shakes her head. She doesn't go in; it would be like entering her brother's bedroom. She waits at the bottom of the steps.

'She fell again on Tuesday. Got out of bed before her knees were ready. Didn't she tell you?'

Jim shakes his head.

'She lay there for an hour before she could crawl to the phone. I think she needs to come and live with me, but she'll hate it. She'll hate me.'

Jim nods. 'She's not right out there, is she? Shall I come with you?'

'Well, what do you think?'

He shrugs, and then says, 'Well, yeah, she'll hate it, but she has to. I'll come with you. Give me two secs.' He shuts the door.

Suzie waits outside while Jim gets dressed. She turns away to watch children gathering on the grass outside the caravans. It's early, but they're emerging from their doorways in various states of undress. Some in crocs and dressing gowns, some in hoodies and jeans.

A little kid with scruffy short hair is wearing a vest, joggers, and school shoes, his head down. He walks quickly, hands in his pockets, a plastic bag swinging from his wrist. He looks more serious than the others, and she wonders why he isn't wearing more clothes. She shivers at the thought of him walking around in just a vest.

Jim pokes his head out of the caravan door.

'Can I just grab a cuppa?' he says. 'Rough night, like.'

'Course. I'm in no rush.'

'Don't know where Jay is. Must've gone out walking again,' Jim mutters, before turning and going back in to make the tea. The caravan door slams behind him, and Suzie sits at a picnic bench to wait, watching the little boy cross the green and disappear into one of the caravans.

LATER, they walk down the road to the spit, Suzie's heart drumming in her chest, her palms sweating, slightly.

Why doesn't her brother ever take the weight of the burden? Why is it always down to her? Her decisions, her suggestions and ultimately, her responsibility?

'Hi Mum,' Suzie says when they walk in, going over to give her a hug. 'We need to talk to you.'

Lily is sitting on the sofa by the coffee table, gazing out to sea. Her mum turns and looks at her sadly, like she already knows what's coming, and that she'd never be the one to say it. And Suzie, weighed down with worry, knows she'll be the one who has to. She sits down on the sofa opposite her mother and takes a breath.

'Will you think about coming to live with me?'

She reaches for her hand, but Lily moves away, tetchily. Suzie knows her mum doesn't want to be looked after and would rather anything than become a burden.

'Damn this stupid old body,' she says. 'I suppose I had better. But I've got so much to do,' she says, looking around her in agitation.

'I know you don't want to.'

'It's probably for the best, Mum,' Jim chips in. 'Keep you safe.'

He's standing in the doorway, one foot already out of the door.

'But I don't want to be safe,' Lily says, in a small voice.

Jim pecks her on the cheek, and then goes off to put some WD-40 on her creaky door handle.

It isn't easy, living with Lily. She's bored and tetchy in the flat. It feels like they are on each other's toes, even though Suzie is out at the shop all day. They bicker, but Suzie never wanted it to be like that. She wanted to come to her mum free woman to free woman, but Lily is no longer that person, living as she pleases, out on the edge of the world.

As the days tick by, Suzie feels more and more like she has broken her mum's spirit. She doesn't know how to fix it and fusses around her, asking incessant questions. Jim, being Jim, manages to get away with being aloof, not taking the responsibility and not shouldering the blame.

Some days, Lily sits with Suzie in the shop, chatting to her and the customers, but it feels like they are just treading water. Suzie's whole life is a bit like that, she realises. She runs the shop just for something to do. What has she given the last five years of her life in service to? A sugar rush, that was all.

Restless in the flat's captivity, Lily regresses. Suzie keeps telling herself it is for the best, but what does she know? Suzie knows there had been another option. She could have gone to live at the beach house. But she didn't raise it and neither did her mum.

Suzie had never liked it there; she was too scared of the edge. It was so open to the elements, so see-through. There was nowhere to hide.

10

ELSIE

Wednesday 8th September 2021

IN THE PINK and quiet morning, Elsie walks around the land, claiming it for her own. She walks along the creeks, knee deep in mist, seeking to understand what this place is trying to tell her. Bernie, her little dog, runs along beside her.

There is an almost imperceptible shift happening, like the ripple of a tide breaking ever so slowly. An edge setting itself up.

September is the month of change, and it thrills her a little, the way that the birds count out the days on their feathers, the way that they hold the whole of the turning year in their feathery grasp, and understand it, as small as they are, as light as they are.

Ten volunteers have arrived at the reserve for the September count, stationing themselves in different areas and counting the roosting birds, before they rise with the dawn. Even when the world is falling apart, you've got to count the birds. The marsh is filling up for September, the month of migration, with thousands of birds using it as a short stay hotel. They are all on their way south for the coming winter.

'Oh, to be a bird,' she sighs. 'All the freedom in the world.'

Later on, Elsie sits down with her strong black coffee, pulls her chair up to the desk and looks out towards the deserted marsh beyond. She begins to compile the data. The Whimbrel are back; 950 counted by the team. They'd be here a few weeks and then off to Africa to bask in the sun over winter. She'd heard them on her rounds this morning, full of chatter as they waded and rested.

There is a flock of Egrets on the freshwater grazing marsh. Wigeon, Avocet, Brent Geese have all been spotted in good numbers. Good for them that they could all get out of the UK.

With the turn of the season and the chill in the morning, their soft bodies know it is time to move on. They will be on their way in a few days. No walls for them.

Take us with you, she thinks, *please don't leave us here.* And as detached as she is from the others, she feels the longing for a change.

11

SUZIE

M onday 13th September 2021

IT'S BEEN a month and Lily still can't settle. She misses the old house.

When Suzie is at the shop, she gets a constant barrage of texts.

I NEED to go back to the house. It's time to go back.
Suzie sighs, taps back
Fine. I'll see if Jim can take you.
Ok. he replies.

JIM CALLS Suzie from the beach house, later, just as she's locking up the shop.

'She's gone, Suz,' he says, and turning, Suzie drops her keys to the floor.

She runs all the way there.

'WE JUST WALKED IN,' he explains later. 'It smelled musty, and the wind was howling in at the back door. It was creaking again, and I said to her, "Oh I'll fix that, Mum, before I go". Parked her up in her wheelchair, just by her old sofa, light streaming in, and then I went out the back to connect up the gas cannister to fix up a cup of tea. Must have been out there for ten minutes, if that. I came back in to put the kettle on. I shouted out "Mum, do you still take one sugar?" And she didn't answer.

'Looked up and could just see the back of her head, just looked like she was looking out at the ocean. I called out to her again. And I went over to her and touched her shoulder. And she'd gone. It's almost like she knew it was coming, like she decided for herself.'

Suzie listens to him telling it back, in disbelief.

It doesn't seem possible that her mother had chosen to die, was able to turn off her own life support, just like that.

'But I didn't say goodbye,' Suzie says, fiddling with the hem of her top, and then turning to the window, to the terrible and empty sea that fills the house with its water. That fills her too now, to overflowing.

There's something about the house, the way it plays with life and death. Shell had been here, hadn't she, the day before she went? What did it tempt her to do? Suzie shivers.

Her mother is still sitting there, propped up in her wheelchair, staring ahead into the emptiness of the sea. Suzie takes hold of her mothers' cold hand, while the paramedics busy themselves around them, looking at the time, filling in forms.

Suzie closes the shop for a day for the funeral. There's only a handful of them there: Suzie, Jim and Jay, and Mike, Jill and Pam – three of Lily's neighbours. After the service, they walk along the spit and out to the beach house. Suzie finds a bottle of Cava hiding in the back of her mum's cupboard and they open it as the sun goes down. It feels peaceful but Suzie is still left filled with sadness and confusion. What she'd give for one last conversation with her mum.

Jill suggests they each toast Lily with some memory or some way to say goodbye, and Suzie says, 'Mum, I just wish we could have had one last chat.' Jill puts her arm around Suzie, and says, 'She wanted to go, but she couldn't have told you because she knew it would break your heart. It was out of love.'

Her words cut across Suzie's whirling mind. They set things straight. She'd remember that. She'd hold on to it, she thought. It was out of love.

Jim looks out to sea, his jaw fixed, his glass raised. Shakes his head when it is his turn to speak. Just takes a sip of Cava and his eyes brim with tears.

Jay holds up his glass timidly, sweeps his hair out of his eyes, says 'Gran, you were always wild and free,' and then takes a slurp out of his glass.

12

THE BIRDS

F riday 17th September 2021

THE STARLINGS CALL to one another at dusk.
    They gather, flock and twirl over the Swale,
    the swirling, rushing river.

OVER THE CHANNEL, up from Mother Europe,
    over to the small island where the wind blows in,
    where the people don't look up enough.

THEY HAVE BEEN CALLED, though,
    by someone who knew they would come.

.   .   .

'LOOK UP,' the starlings cry, as they gather,
    'Look up! We know how to be free!' they call into the wind,
    as they loop and squawk and dive.

BUT AS THEY CALL OUT, they lament
    as they see the stragglers, the ones walking home,
    the swimmers, the lost ones, the boys at the park,
    the ones drifting silently out to sea,
    the mums crying into the kitchen sink,
    or sitting with glazed eyes while their baby cries and cries,
    the dads opening a can of beer
    because there is no way they can talk about it,
    trotting off to work with a heart as heavy as a stone
    because there is no other choice.
    They see the broken-hearted grans and grandads
    who don't see their grandchildren anymore,
    the weary and bone-tired ones,
    the ones with no family,
    the depressed and unlovable ones.

'WE HAVE TO DO SOMETHING,' the starlings murmur,
    feather crossing feather,
    their iridescent streaks of beauty twirling
    in the falling dusk.

'SO BEAUTIFUL AS WE ARE, beautiful they must be.'

· · ·

THERE IS A MURMURATION OF DISSENT,
        quickly quelled by the others.
        'The whole sky belongs to us; who says we can't?'

AND AS THEY fly as one, their thoughts become one,
        and the tiny collisions begin, all over the place.

13

SUZIE

Saturday 18th September 2021

SUZIE FLICKS on the heating and lets Rocky outside to do his business. It's Saturday night and the evenings are turning colder already. Two more weeks until she closes up for the year. She settles down with another re-run of The Great British Bake Off, Rocky curling up alongside her.

She can't settle, though, and thinks about Mum and the beach house, and wonders if she could ever make it her home. She and Jim grew up with their mother and father up on the north of the island, but their father left them long ago, when Suzie was five and Jim was even younger. Met some lady who'd come to the island on holiday, Pat, said he'd fallen in love with her, said he couldn't help himself. After he left, Suzie didn't see him for years, although he still sent a card for her birthday each year. Whenever she recognised his writing on the envelope, her heart would twist, and she would be overcome with indecision. *Should I go and see him? Should I make up with him? Is this all my fault or his?* So, it was a relief when the cards stopped coming. But then there was a letter from Pat, saying he had died, that there was a funeral.

None of them went. When he was gone, he was gone. But he was the one who had chosen it. Not her.

After Suzie and Jim left home, Mum saw the beach house come up for sale and moved down there mortgage-free, tried to live off the land, off thin air, growing her own veg and all. So the house out on the spit was never Suzie's. She'd slept there a few times, and almost came under its spell. But she had never liked waking there, with the curtainless windows full of the gaze of the sea. It made her feel vulnerable, naked. But that was exactly why her mother loved it – she came alive there.

Suzie was so proud of her mother's transformation. She could've been one of those women who just waited around to die, but she didn't. She turned herself into someone else and crafted a life that she loved. So how could they sell the house, when it was Lily's soul laid down in wood and sand?

From October till May, Suzie's days will sink into the same ritual: wake, tidy the flat, take Rocky for a walk, get back, have lunch. She tries not to watch the TV in the day to begin with, but then the rain comes, and the cold and she gives in. Winter numbs her right down, and the TV soothes her pain. It happens every year. The rhythm holds and discomforts her at the same time.

Sometimes, when she can't sleep, she imagines dying alone. Some days she realises that there isn't anyone who would text to invite her to the pub quiz or check up on her if she didn't show up for work. Maybe Jim would, after a while.

Every time something had gone wrong, when her dad ran off, when Trish broke her heart, when Mum died, part of her snapped off inside until all that was left was a jumble of broken shards. She would never impose that on to someone else. Who else would want to know?And then it strikes her like a punch in the chest. Trish is the love of her life. No man has ever come close. That's why she left a cavernous hole when she moved away and that's why Suzie's whole life seemed to be an arc straining towards her still.

The very thing she praised her Mum for was the very opposite of the thing that she was doing herself. Why couldn't she get over Trish and what she had done to her? Why was her life still on hold, after all these years? Maybe because Trish had done the exact same thing that her dad had done; she had let their relationship fall into the abyss and claim it had nothing to do with her. She had stolen Jonathan, the only one who had ever liked her.

Suzie turns off the television and starts pacing around the flat. She stands at the window, watching the rain snake its way down the windowpane, lit by the orange streetlamp outside. A storm has come on quickly. She can feel a rising anger.

'I've got to get out of here,' she says. 'I've got to change something.'

She puts on her leggings and trainers and runs out of her flat and down to the beach, taking Rocky with her, even though it is nearing 10pm. She doesn't normally do this kind of thing.

They run down to the sea-front, in the dark, with the streetlights shining. The rain pelts down and the sea crashes on to the shore. She runs as far as she can, up to Warden, the next village up the coast. When she gets there, she bends over to catch her breath, holding her knees, feeling her heart pounding within her. She wishes she had bought something to drink.

'Come on Rocky,' she shouts, and runs down to the sea where she splashes her face with the cold icy water.

He barks and they start back the way they came, along the beach now, dodging in and out of the inky waves.

She gets back to her flat and is buzzing. Her fingers are numb from the cold. Her chest is tight from the night air. She drinks a whole glass of water, then runs a shower and stands in the steam. She feels alive, like she hasn't for a long time.

What is it that's changed? Herself. Nothing more, nothing less. Perhaps if she could see herself as precious, then other people would too. Funny, the way things go, the day things change.

It is as if something has been switched on inside of her.

As if some part of her has just woken up.

14

JAY

Sunday 19th September 2021

I WAKE and look outside where the pavements are glistening from a recent rainfall. I take it as a challenge. I want to go out and be alive in it, whatever it looks like.

'Just popping out for a walk, Dad,' I call, as I open the door and let it fall shut behind me. I scoop up the binbag that had been chucked out on the front step the night before and walk off towards the caravan park bins.

It's a foul morning. A cold and cruel storm is still raging, which is rare for September. The wind blows into my hoodie, hollowing me out. I will have to leave Dad. I've not really thought about it with such finality before, with such clarity. But there it is. One last year of college left, and then I'm out of here.

I throw the binbag into the bin and set off towards the

footpath down to the sea edge, running down the track to somehow get the storm into my lungs.

A little kid darts out from a caravan in a white vest. His hair is kind of messy and matted, and even from a way off I can see his face is grubby. He watches me from the side of the path. As I come level with him, he runs in front of me, and I have to stop dead so as to not take him out altogether. He holds out his stick gun to me.

'I'm Kit,' he says.

'Kit, you need to watch where yer going!'

He shrugs and runs off.

It strikes me as strange that he's running around at 8.15 in a vest, on his own on a stormy Sunday morning. It is cold. He has a carrier bag in his hand from the Sunny convenience store, with a few things in it.

'Hey, where's your mum?' I call after him.

He turns and shrugs, and then disappears into a bush.

I stare after him for a while and then walk on. Nothing to do with me, I think. I've got enough to deal with.

I pull up my hood, put my headphones in my ears and set off.

I end up down on the shore, walking along by the breakers, up towards Warden.

Our little island—pushed out into the Thames estuary, in the crook of the arm of Europe, so close that we could almost see her—is at sea. Feels like the island is a boat of migrants, weighed so far down with sorrow that it's almost sinking. The rim of the boat is getting closer to the surface of the water, and as soon as the water breaches it, it will pool in, and we will all go under.

The rain has stopped. The grey sky still looms but there's a kind of brightness shining through. A hint of a rainbow up by the empty mini-golf course. The gulls scream as if the entire sea belongs to them. In summer, they pull chip packets from overflowing bins, and pick up discarded bags of candy floss, left by young revellers. They watch the humans carefully, and then take what they want, screeching with laughter.

In September though, they reclaim this whole place. Leysdown looks like the aftermath of a festival at this time of year. The banners on the strip are all falling down, and the rubbish topples out of bins, blowing this way and that in the wind.

The council workers are slowly putting it all back together – tidying, gathering, clearing, fixing. Gives them something to do through the winter months when no one comes. The place closes down completely over winter. It turns into a ghost town and we all skirt around the edges until next summer.

I walk on and up towards Warden, where the houses are falling down the cliff. The North Sea has been eating away at the land beneath them for several years. Cracks in the roads sometimes appear overnight. Folks are losing their homes to the sea, even now. Sometimes it feels as if the whole island is being swallowed up.

The thought gives me anxiety pangs because what can we do to stop it? There's nothing we can do. You just have to face the other way, looking out to sea, letting the deep blue calm wash over and over and over your fears, even as it eats you alive.

15

———

SUZIE

S unday 19th September 2021

SUZIE WAKES the next morning and thinks, *What now?* She isn't sure quite what has been released in her, but she sure as hell doesn't want to shut it up again.

Before anything else, she knows she needs to feel the exhilaration that she felt last night. She pulls on leggings and a top and scrapes her hair back into a bun. She doesn't care what she looks like. She swallows a full glass of water and sets out.

There's something powerful in her feet pounding on the pavement, some adrenaline thrust in the whole of her heavy body being propelled along by her own power. Something, too, about feeling that ache in her lungs, an ache of use, of being spent. Today, for the first time, she has a sense that her life will take her somewhere after all.

She runs the same way as the night before. Up out of Leysdown and up onto the coast path towards Warden. Down onto the stony beach where the fossils lie hidden.

Her nephew Jay is there, standing against the sea railing, looking out into the wind.

'Hi Jay,' she says.

He jumps.

'Oh hi, Aunty Suz,' he says, and then, looking her up and down, 'I didn't know you ran.'

'Nor did I,' she chuckles. 'Only started last night.'

She breathes heavily, and she can feel her face flushing, but she refuses to feel bad about herself.

Not. Doing. That. Any. More.

'Everyone's got to start somewhere, right? How's yer dad doing?'

Jay shrugs.

'I might wander back with you, if you're going back. Pop by for a cuppa?'

'Yeah sure, I'm heading back now.'

They turn and start to walk back together.

'I've been thinking about next year. Leaving. What Dad will do?' says Jay, trailing off. 'Anyway, where did the running come from?'

'I had this thing, this feeling. Like something came alive in me. I don't know; it was strange.'

Jay looks at her sharply.

'What, like you had suddenly woken up?'

'Yeah, just like that.'

'You do seem different. Lighter somehow?'

She smiles.

'And don't worry about your dad. He'll be fine. I'll keep an eye out for him. You go and live your life, Jay.'

Suzie had tried, many awkward times to talk to Jay about his mum, but he didn't want to talk about it, and she didn't know what to say, so, in the end, she stopped trying.

They walk back together to the caravan park.

'You again!' Jim says, when he sees them.

'Sorry, can't keep away,' Suzie says, her hands raised in protest.

'Cuppa?'

She nods.

'I'm going to go back. I think it's time. Back to the house. What do we do with it though, Jim? Renovate it? Sell it?'

'I don't know, babe,' her brother replies. 'You tell me.'

'Could you bear to sell it?'

He looks into the sky, as if it will give him the answer.

'I don't know if I could. But to be fair, we could probably use the money.'

'Suppose you're right. Wonder what it's even worth. Wonder if anyone's buying houses these days.'

Later, she walks down the long, empty track, carrying a pot of white paint, a brush and some sandpaper. The telegraph poles lean into the wind and the tarmac is eaten up with potholes.

There is a sign saying PRIVATE, NO ENTRY on the gate. She undoes the latch and goes in. The path runs along the back of the houses, but she passes between them and walks down on the sand. She stops to pick up a handful of stones and slips them into her pocket. She walks along the beach to Little Haven, her Mum's house, and unlocks the door.

She thought she might feel a sense of her mum's spirit, lingering, but the house just feels cold and empty.

Nothing has moved since that day.

Jim came back to clear out the kitchen cupboards, but they had left the rest as it was.

Suzie sits on the sofa and imagines her Mum is still there. No memory loss, no arthritis. No Cut Off. She tries to imagine back to that time, but it feels too far away.

The whole house points out to sea and seems to taunt the sea's greatness with its vulnerability, its proximity. It says, 'Come on then,' to the sea, as if a younger brother to an older, or David to Goliath, not knowing the power he tempts.

Suzie death stares the sea. Then she stands and shouts at the top of her lungs, 'Come and get me then!' There *is* something in the house, some spirit. It makes her unafraid and she takes its mantel upon her, takes its boldness right into her being.

'Why didn't I listen to you Mum, all those years ago? Why didn't I see how brave you had already been?' she whispers.

The thought crosses her mind that perhaps her mum would still be here now if she hadn't meddled with her life, cut across her will and bought her to live in Leysdown. She was trying to do the right thing, though. Was it the right thing?

She cries then, for Mum. For Shellie. For Trish. For all that has been lost.

The house grows dark and the cold creeps in. Suzie hadn't meant to stay so long, but now that she is there, at one with the house, she doesn't want to leave. There's bedding there, and she could stay but she hasn't brought anything for dinner and Rocky will be missing her. So, she waits a little longer, until it is quite dark and then stands to leave. As she does, she sees the pot of paint, the brush, the sandpaper. *Oh yes, the painting*, she thinks.

It had just been an excuse to get herself there.

She runs all the way home, feeling lighter than she has

in a long time, the thud of her feet on the pavement carrying her.

16

ELSIE

T uesday 21st September 2021

ELSIE GRAYLING SITS in her faded burgundy armchair, re-reading *Silent Spring* by Rachel Carson. She worries all year round about whether the birds will come back, the reasons for the silent spring, and how carefully we are balanced, woman and beast.

Her thoughts always circle back to the reserve, her beating heart, to the unstable summers and winters, and to how the habitat must be managed. She, as warden, has a duty to make it a safe space for the birds, and countless thousands are spent on the pipes and drains, which manage the water levels in the reserve. The birds won't come if it is too dry. But there's been a letter announcing drastic cuts to future funding. And if that were to happen, the birds wouldn't come. Something has to change now. Before everything falls apart.

Today there is a restlessness, an adrenaline buzz in her fingers. They feel numb to the touch.

'It's time, Bernie. I'm sure of it.'

She goes up to the top of the house and looks out. The skies are still. Blue. There is a sharp chill in the air already, unusual for September.

Bernie follows and whimpers under the weight of her cold hand. She pulls the windows shut and goes downstairs to the study, where the remnants of a log still glow in the burner.

She unscrews her metal percolator and fills the bottom half with water and the middle section with ground coffee. She turns on the computer as she listens to the water bubble up and smells the scent of coffee rise and fill the house.

She gave in to the internet ten years ago and she knows it has its uses, but it feels like white noise to her, too. A mass of information fighting for her attention.

She uses it mostly for the RSPB survey and for putting up blog posts for her handful of subscribers. She's started writing about the things that change, the things she notices. She wants to chronicle them somehow, the almost imperceptible changes. She calls the blog *Sceapig*, the old English name for the island.

Today, though, she has a story to post. She takes her hot coffee and sits at her desk to read through the story one last time. It'd been featured in an obscure literary journal in the 70s, but no one knew what she was talking about back then. No one saw it as a foreshadowing, just as fantasy.

She makes a few tiny tweaks, a comma here, a dash there, but it's her story, and it is true. She has known it for so many years. She has rewritten it so many times.

This time, the words leap up and grab her by the throat.

They are urgent, she knows. But this adrenaline buzz, this pounding heart tells her it is soon, it is now.

She didn't know when it would happen, only that it was coming.

So, in her little corner of the internet, she posts her story.

It has wings, she's confident of that, and it will find the right people; the ones who need to hear. And later, after all of this is over, anyone searching for a certain phrase will also find it. It is the answer to everything. She sits there looking out at the sun sinking down and spreading its glory all over the marshes.

Elsie has known for a long time that there was something special about the birds – some predicament that we couldn't rescue ourselves from. Some work that we couldn't do that they were carrying out, on our behalf.

'Strange shepherds, us island ones,' she says, looking through the cracked and dirty pane to the glory beyond. 'Leading the people in a way they don't know.'

There's an essay she's written, and she posts that too. *They'll need a little background information if they are going to understand*, she thinks, *if they are going to piece together the clues.*

'It is about living vital lives,' she wrote in the essay; that was the lesson of the birds, and the lesson that her life had taught her. 'People fail you. Only the birds are safe. Live vital lives. Are you awake? Are you living for something essential?'

Elsie's parents were hard people, with not much love to give. But now she sees she had to choose to love herself. *If I don't care for myself, then who will?* was the lesson she had learned over the years as she shed the skin of people pleasing, of fitting in, of keeping up appearances, of comparison.

She sees the young ones these days, sucked into their black mirrors, always looking down instead of looking up. It was the biggest shepherd, and it was herding them into the smallest room in the world – the room of the self. She often thinks: *If only they knew.*

And then, in the glowing pink of dusk, she hears the faint noise that she knows so well, that her bones know, and it startles something awake in her.

It is the noise of thousands of wings, beating at once.

She pulls her reading glasses from her face and walks over to the window.

'They've come back,' she murmurs. 'I knew it. I told you Bernie.'

The adrenaline sets her heart beating in its old cage and the palpitations make her breathe faster, make her feel the dizzying pull of hope again, of first love, somehow.

'Hope,' she whispers, 'is the thing with feathers.'

And despite herself and her steely nature, a tear escapes from her eye, her heart, and rolls down her cheek.

A tear of relief. She hadn't got it wrong; she had heard.

'If the starlings have come back, so many and so soon,' Elsie says, 'it means it is time. The vital principle has been awakened. They have come to take us, us trapped Sceapig islanders, marooned as we are, inside our tall Cut Off wall.

'Their voice has always been there, quietly whispering, quietly lamenting, and those who have stilled themselves and who are waiting for more will hear, if they choose to. They come to cull but also to wake. They have a poison, but also the grace to say wake up to those who have not seen, I am sure of it. It is time,' she whispers, her heart trilling away in her chest.

You'd sometimes see them, the starlings, high up, or a

few, flitting on the wind, but it was this almighty gathering that she had been longing for, all at once, like a whirlwind.

They gather, swirl, and loop, and she feels akin to God. She feels sure they will take her.

As she stands there with the thousands of birds circling her strange, tall house, and the windows open so she can hear the flapping of their wings, she feels sure she will be raptured.

She holds her arms held out to the sides, her eyes closed, feeling the pull of the heavens, of bird-land. She trembles, as she imagines it, the pulling of her soul aloft, the transforming of her cold, bony frame into something light, agile, hollow-boned.

'Oh, to be a bird,' she sobs.

It is all she wants.

But instead of the rapture she so craves, the sound of the flapping wings around the house lessens and quietens down, until she can no longer hear the rush of their wings.

Bernie whines and scratches at the door. She lets him in and then hurries back to the window. She can see the dark cloud of them dancing away across the island, north, towards Leysdown.

'Come back,' she whispers. 'I want you to take me.'

She runs outside into the dusk, but wishes instead that she had run upstairs, to the top of the house, where she could be nearer to the birds, to their flight and thrust.

She stands there as the wings of the dusk settle down, the pink glow spreading all over the marshes, the pools of light reflecting the rose-gold sky.

Tears roll down her cheeks as she turns to watch them go. She is emptied out, a shell of wanting.

'Come back,' she cries, into the dusk.

. . .

SHE TURNS and a boy is there.

He is standing on the path, where no one walks, and he is watching her. She has seen him before. It is the boy from the other day.

He wears a dirty grey hoodie, and his hair is long and tucked behind his ears. He watches her as if he knows he shouldn't, but there is nowhere to hide out here, so he just stands there. His skin is quietly illuminated by the dusk.

Elsie is affronted at another human being in her private place. She always assumes it is just her, and is surprised, sometimes, to remember that there are other human beings on the planet.

'The birds,' she says, distractedly, pointing after them. 'I was watching ...'

There is something different about this one. He is present. He is really there. Tied to the land or something. He is waiting for something.

'I saw them too,' the boy says, his hands pushed awkwardly into his jeans pockets. 'I've been walking out this way. I saw you in the kitchen yesterday.'

She murmurs, 'You must think I'm a mad thing.'

'No, not at all. I would love to live out here.'

There is a pause where she looks at him, considers him.

'You aren't like the others,' she says. 'Do you want to stop for a coffee?'

The boy, without appearing to realise how honoured he is, accepts. Elsie hasn't invited anyone to spend time with her for years.

Elsie gestures to the bench and her new companion sits.

'I'm Jay' he says. She nods and disappears into the house.

'Milk? Sugar?' she calls through the doorway.

'Both please.'

· · ·

ELSIE RETURNS with two coffees in enamel mugs, steaming in the dusk. Bernie runs along next to her.

'This is Bernie,' she says. 'He's my keeper.'

Jay is looking up at her back wall, and Elsie can see what he's thinking.

'It looks like someone has lifted the house clear out of a town and placed it here, doesn't it? It was for the cement works, all gone now.'

He nods.

They sit in the yard – the fenced off area surrounded by marshland, the steam from the scalding coffee rising between them. Elsie wonders why she has invited a teenage boy to have coffee with her, and by the look on Jay's face, he is wondering why he said yes.

'Aren't you scared?' Jay asks, suddenly. 'Out here on your own? Just this little wall to protect you?"

'Oh no,' she laughs. 'What could hurt me out here? It's the humans you have to watch out for.'

'I know that well enough,' Jay mutters, taking a mouthful of coffee, scalding his tongue.

The wind rushes over the marsh, cooling the coffee in their hands. Elsie leans towards Jay and whispers, 'There's something about you.'

She pauses and then adds, 'Do you want to know the way of the birds?'

Jay nods. 'They are the only thing that make sense now, aren't they?'

Elsie's eyes brim with tears.

'Yes, they are. You've got the silence in you. I can see it. You are quiet enough to hear.'

Where is all this emotion coming from, she wonders?

'I'll teach you if you want to come. I've lived out here for forty-two years now. Know these birds like the back of my hand.'

She chuckles like a thing set free and slurps a mouthful of coffee.

'I've got time now' he says, with a shrug.

Elsie smiles a wry smile. 'You understand, too, that there is little time left then?'

He nods.

'Well let's start with what we see. September is the month of change. The birds use this place as a hotel, so many coming and going. Can you hear that high whistle?'

Jay nods.

'That's the Golden Plover. He'll be on his way soon. There's a pair of barn owls who have made a nest in the old barn. You will see their white bodies swooping low across the marsh at dusk. The Marsh Harriers are the kings of the place, of course. It's all theirs for the taking. It's the starlings though that we must watch. Did you see them just now? They are too many, it's too early. They don't normally come until late October; they are trying to tell us something, I am sure of it.'

'Yes, I saw them. So beautiful,' Jay says.

'They are.' Elsie smiles. 'And so close, and you didn't even know it.' She looks Jay straight in the eyes and sends him a different message, whispered into his heart: 'Wake up.'

She sees it come to him like a shock, like a breath of morning air.

17

JAY

Friday 24th September 2021

DAD STANDS AT THE WORKTOP, buttering his toast.

'Are you waiting for Mum to come back?' I say. 'Because she ain't gonna come back.'

There's impatience in my voice – I've been up all night, thinking about it, figuring it out. Feels like I'm about to burst.

'No, son, I'm not waiting for her.'

'You can't stay here Dad. You're wasting away. Let's just move, go anywhere. I don't care. I'll stay with you.'

'Son. Just leave it will yer?' he says, looking away.

'But Dad!' I'm almost shouting. 'I can't bear to see you doing this to yourself. You're better than this! You're better than just whiling away your days in this hell-hole of a caravan park. PLEASE DAD! I want us to have some hope of a future together.'

My voice breaks, and all that I've held back for so long comes rushing through me like a torrent.

'I just want to imagine that we have a life to live together. Can't we have that? Dad. Dad?' I shout, sobbing through the words.

I think he's more shocked than anything. He stands there and takes it, and then reaches out awkwardly to punch me on the shoulder. I stand in front of him. The tears slow, and I wipe them away and just breathe.

And then I say quietly, 'Just think about it, ok? Fresh start, you and me.'

And I look up and catch his eye and I think he sees me for the first time in years. I see his stubble, his grey hairs, spreading from the sides to the back of his head. He looks tired, but he smiles, and it feels like the tears have punched through a wall somehow.

'A new adventure, eh? I'll think about it.'

And even though I'm not sure he'll ever leave, it lifts my heart a little to hear him say he'll think about it.

'Ok Dad. I'd better go. Sorry,' I say, wiping my nose on my sleeve and quickly making my sandwiches. I open the caravan door and a gust of wind whips it back again.

'Love you Dad,' I call out, as I step out into the wind. 'I'm out for a drink tonight with the boys so I'll be back late, ok?'

The wind catches the door and slams it shut behind me. I don't even hear if he says goodbye.

18

ELSIE

F riday 24th September 2021

ELSIE CREEPS around the reserve in the morning as if she's waiting for something. Her heart beats a little bit faster in anticipation. She looks for the boy, but he is nowhere.

The skeins of cloud are drawn out like wool, and the sky is the most perfect blue. Calm before the storm. She hopes.

Everything is in place. She walks her six-mile loop, and the bird numbers look good, the water levels are good. Everything is right for September, the season of change. They are all tucked under her belt, the rhythms and rhymes of this place – she knows them like old friends.

She has never got tired of this place, but for some reason today, she feels like she is saying goodbye.

She hopes with all of her heart. She hopes so hard that it hurts.

19

————

FEE

F riday 24ᵗʰ September 2021

I DIDN'T HAVE *wings before, but I had always dreamed of them.*
   Father disappeared and I knew that Mother
   would never have done anything about it,
   so scared, as she was, of the government,
   so I knew I had to go instead.
   I couldn't tell her I was leaving
   because she would have stopped me.
   I would do it though, I was sure of it.
   I would go and find him,
   I would bring him back and make it all ok again.
   I wanted it so badly that I knew I had the power to make it
happen.
   What else do we need except to be with the ones that we
love?

.   .   .

I HAD to pass through this way, it was the only way.
And somehow, I willed that bird being right into my bones.
I was there, on the run, in a Travelodge in Southend-on-Sea.
I knew I had to get to Papa, get to the stepping stone island in
the sea
if I was ever going to see him again.
And I can't explain what happened
because I didn't see it from outside of myself.
All I know is, I was carried aloft.
I became light, my bones became hollow.
All my heaviness melted away as the ground left me.

20

SUZIE

F riday 24th September 2021

OUT AT WARDEN, Suzie shivers and looks up at the indigo sky. A sudden urge has come over her to run and keep running, to contain this island in her pocket. To own it, to feel big against its beating heart, this pebble flung into the sea.

She can hear the far-off voices of teenagers shouting in the darkness. She feels a kinship with the night now, as if she owns it. She is unafraid. She pauses at the summit of the hill and moves on, down towards Shellness, the dark hamlet perched on the edge of the world.

21

ELSIE

F riday 24th September 2021

ELSIE IS ready for them this time. Her windows are wide open, and she is watching. She has been waiting all day and into the evening.

She hears them approach, faintly, faintly, coming up from the south, and then she sees them come into focus. She sees more and more gather, the multitude coming together, and even in the darkness, lit by moonlight, she sees their oneness.

Tears fall from her eyes, and she closes them for a moment so she can feel the wind shift, feel the feathered bodies moving as one, communicating in a way that humans can only guess at.

They enfold her house, her whole life, with their rushing, tumbling flight.

Her old friends, the starlings, are back, whirling around

her house, turning her very being into the eye of their tornado. She lifts up her hands in exhilaration at being remembered by them.

For so long she has waited.

And they came, finally, like she always knew they would.

Outside, the starlings move as one black body, one suit of armour, creaking and squawking as a thousand wings turn.

Elsie is in reverie; she turns as they encircle the house.

'It is time, it is time,' she cries out.

AND AS SURELY AS she says it, a blanket of starlings flies in through the window and wrap around her. They smother her in a cloak of black and when they fly out again all that is left are the clothes she was wearing, crumpled into a heap on the floor: her shirt and camo trousers, her socks, her cotton knickers, her bra. Her glasses. All the things that hold her up, that make her, her.

BERNIE WHIMPERS IN THE NIGHT, and the empty house groans as the wind runs through it. He pulls Elsie's still-warm shirt from the heap in the middle of the bedroom and carries it over to the corner, behind the bed, a little sheltered from the wind. He cowers in the corner of the bedroom, her shirt beneath his paws, waiting for her to return.

The wind blows the curtains in and combs through her things, rustling the papers on the desk, spilling them out upon the floor.

22

PETE

F riday 24th September 2021

EVEN THOUGH HE shut up early, Pete has only just got back to the caravan, what with cleaning down, cashing up, antibacing the whole place. He still feels dodgy as hell but can't turn in without a bit of telly. A Match of the Day rerun will sort him out before bed, a light bit of banter. Of course, it makes him miss the Prem. It folded as soon as the borders closed – the clubs couldn't run without superstars, the punters couldn't afford the games.

He's not sure what's wrong. It feels like a fluttering in his chest, or his heart beating slightly out of time. He feels breathless but isn't going to be soft about it. He'll be fine after a good night's sleep.

A noise outside catches his attention.

'What on earth?' he says, squinting to see past the blinds. He takes a quick slurp of tea and burns his tongue.

It sounds like an earthquake rumbling... no, it's not earth-bound, more like something massive hovering just outside. A tornado? It is a sound that he doesn't know. He walks to the door of the caravan and throws it open. There is a screeching blackness, and he cries out, instinctively covering his face, dropping his scalding mug of tea on the floor.

There are a thousand wings – claws scratching, feathers flapping. He slams the door shut and stands with his back to it, clutching the sink with his left hand and the coat cupboard with his right, pressing his back up against the glass as if the sheer mass of them could break down his door now that they have seen him.

His chest is heaving, and he strives to control his breathing and resist the urge to pass out. He gets that sharp ache again, over to the left. He knows it's his heart.

He has never seen so many birds. What are they doing out there in the dark?

His thoughts fly: *Don't they do the roosting thing earlier in the day? Birds don't swarm, do they?* That's wasps. Maybe he's had one too many ales tonight. They can't be coming after him, can they? What has he ever done to them? Why are they trying to get into his caravan?

Pete sinks down to the floor and sits there with his back against the door, trying to figure it out. He concentrates on keeping his breathing nice and steady. His heart skips along at double time. The fact that his door is made of frosted glass is freaking him out. They'll be able to see him against the door. But they're only birds; they aren't that clever, are they? Why are they coming for him?

'Just keep it locked, Pete,' he says to himself. 'They'll move on.'

He's always found something terrifying about mass

numbers – of any kind of beast: ants, bees, birds. The thought of a swarm gives him goosebumps. The fact that a man could be overrun by something so small, so breakable. But swarms always win. The strength is in the multitude.

He shudders, crawls up onto his knees to make sure the door is locked and bolted and then crawls back to the sofa. What a night.

Perhaps he needs one more to take the edge off. There is a bottle of homebrew in the fridge – he just has to get there. He crawls back to the door to double check it's bolted and then continues over to open the fridge door. He edges slowly backwards to the sofa cradling his ice-cold brew. He doesn't want to stand in case they see his shadow.

There is the sound of something hitting the glass, something soft and full.

Pete's terrified. He's never been so scared in his life. He sips the home brew slowly, trying to still his heart.

He crawls to the corner table where a lamp shines out a pool of orange light. He flicks off the lamp before returning to the door, where he peers through the frosted glass. There's a dark lump on the top step.

He's had enough of this. On hands and knees he heads to the bedroom, too tired to take a slash, and buries himself under the covers and tries to sleep. But the soft thumps continue, and he knows the birds are dive bombing his front door, its frosted pane being chipped away at constantly. What do they want with him?

He falls into a fitful slumber until another thump jolts him awake again. In a moment of bold stupidity, he gets up, unlocks the door, and yanks it open, yelling, 'WHAT? WHAT DO YOU WANT?' at the birds.

But the moment he pulls back the door they swarm into the caravan, like he knew they would, swallowing its beige interior with the mass of their flapping, iridescent feathers and beady eyes. They devour his body with their beaks, pulling flesh from his arms and legs. And then, sweet mercy, they peck his heart right out of his chest. He watches a group of them carry it up and away with them, out of the door. He tries to shriek, 'No! Give it back, it's my heart!' but his voice doesn't come out.

As soon as they've extracted his heart, the weight lifts and the flapping and pecking stops. They lift away from him and fly out of the door as though they have got what they came for.

And then there is only silence, apart from the door flapping on its hinge and banging against the metal caravan. In the indigo darkness, Pete can hear the birds coming and going across the caravan park. He daren't move for some time. He just lies there, wriggling his fingers, checking he's still alive. The door bangs against the rail and a fresh gust of wind makes him shiver.

He slowly raises a hand to his chest and feels it. He checks his arms, where the birds were pulling away at his skin, but they look normal. He wonders if it were all a dream, or one too many bad beers from the pub? Is he still alive? He reaches up to his chest and can feel a scar from his collar bone down to his third rib. It feels warm and raised, like a line of solder. But why is he still alive? And what have they done to him? If they have taken his heart, what is he left with, and what can he feel now, beating so fast beneath the thin drum of his skin?

23

SUZIE

Friday 24th September 2021

Suzie is running, running, running in the darkness, her head torch on, little Rocky at her heel. She hears a rushing noise and then suddenly it is all around her, the flapping, feathered iridescence.

But it doesn't slow her down, it propels her faster.

The birds and their feathered wings carry her aloft, they make a staircase for her up to the indigo sky. She can feel all the power of their thousand wings in her legs and she wants to be every part of this and more.

Rocky looks up into the deepening sky in confusion. He runs along on the tarmac of the esplanade, barking up at her.

But Suzie doesn't look back.

This is her and she is it, at one with the power of the multitude.

Strong. Determined. Beautiful.
She doesn't want anything else.
She runs on and on.

24

———

FEE

Friday 24th September 2021

AND THEN, *as I gain weight,*
and fall into place in this strange land,
all these other ones.
The forms of their slumbering bodies, are taken,
lifted high into the night,
into the chattering caress of the feathered ones.
As they are lifted, they become lighter,
and their skin sprouts feathers.
It is so beautiful that I can't stand it.
All of their sadness falls away from them as they float,
weightless.

BUT I AM CALLED *for something else, and it is to change the tide.*

I know I have to get to Papa, to get to old Europe, the
European Free Republic,
    to pull these countries together again.

THE BIRDS MUST KNOW, *they must know it is necessary*
    otherwise, why would they help me?
    Perhaps this is the only way.
    I wonder why me, but there is no time for that
    and I accept the gift for what it is.
    I settle down into my human bones again,
    and wait for morning.

25

JAY

Saturday 25th September 2021

AFTER

I STAND THERE, staring around at the caravan park. Kids are crying, wandering outside half-dressed.

Rob and Ava are looking at me expectantly, as if I should know what to do next.

I take a rationed ciggy from my pack and close my eyes for a moment. I try to light it, but my hands are trembling.

'Hang on,' I say, over my shoulder to Rob and Ava. 'I'm sorry. I just need to think for a minute.'

I smoke slowly, looking at the children – the panic and the novelty of it. Some are walking hand in hand between the caravans, ignoring the drone of continual crying coming from inside. Some kids are hugging, some are playing tag.

There are little ones who can't unlock their doors. I can see them now, their tiny faces pressed up at the windows, the net curtains pulled aside to watch everything unfold.

'So, what are we gonna do?' Rob says, insistently.

I don't know why he thinks I know.

'Erm... Keep doing what you're doing, I guess? Go back to your house, and gather everyone else you can find. Look after the little ones.'

Robin is one of the few people I know who still lives in an actual house, on a real road. It had belonged to his Gran, and when she died she left it to his mum, so there was no chance of it being taken from her.

'If you can fit them all in, that is ... then maybe find some other teenagers to gather some. Who's the oldest person you've seen?'

He shrugs.

'Us.'

The silence then. Between me, as I try to take it all in, Rob, who is still as white as a ghost, and Ava, whose shoulders are shuddering again with quiet tears.

'Well ...' my mind is running away with itself, so I speak calmly and slowly. 'I should stay at the caravan park. There are babies here. I need to make sure everyone's safe.'

Rob nods. 'Ok. You do that and ... I guess we meet up later? Say five, in the playground?'

'Yes,' I say. 'Ok. Have you seen Swanny?'

'He was riding his bike around the estate this morning. He looked wild. I don't know if he was scared or high or something.'

'We'll deal with him later.' When Rob doesn't move I say, 'Go! Kids are going to die today if we don't find them.'

Rob and Ava walk away, then they jog, then they start to run.

I'm left alone, and the caravan park is starting to look like a refugee camp for kids. One stares at me through the locked window of her home, and I know I have to get them all out but it's nine a.m. and I'm exhausted already. I go inside my own caravan, and sit on the bed my heart pounding, my head reeling.

If Dad had gone, he would have left a note, wouldn't he?

How can he be gone? How can they all be gone? It can't be true.

I feel sick to the pit of my stomach. My whole body starts to tremble and I hold my head in my hands. The tears come; I can't help it.

'Dad,' I cry. 'Dad, I need you.'

After a few minutes, a sense of calm washes over me.

I'll just do what I can, like anyone would. I have no choice to hide away. No matter how sick to the stomach I am with fear.

I go back outside, take a deep breath and walk towards the first two children I see.

'Have you guys had any breakfast?'

They shake their heads.

'Mum and Dad have gone out.'

I nod.

'Seems like all the mums and dads have gone out. Let's just have a walk shall we, and then we'll get everyone to come back to my caravan for breakfast.'

They nod, and I take the boy's hand and we knock at each door, one by one. Some of them are locked, so I take a brick and smash the windows of the ones we can't get into. We search every bedroom. The kids all help. Out of a hundred caravans, there are sixty-six children. Too many for my caravan. I grab as many duvets as I can carry, and we make a big rug on the green.

'Right,' I start, addressing the group. 'I don't know what is going on. I don't know where the mums and dads have gone. But I need you to all be very grown up, ok? We all need to help each other. Until we find all the grown-ups, we are one big family. We are the Leysdown Holiday Park family now, ok?'

I look out to the sea of shell-shocked kids. Some are vaguely nodding back at me.

'I want you to all shout out your names,' I say, scribbling them down on a piece of paper as they do. I make my way through the group, writing down all the details I can get out of them.

As I write, I wonder what it's for and who I'm going to tell.

There is one baby, a six-month-old, who, as it stands, isn't screaming, so we're in a good place. There's also a baby who looks about one, crawling around, putting everything in his mouth, an older child following, anxiously.

'Ok,' I call out. 'Who's good with babies?'

A girl I recognise from the park, who looks about fourteen-ish, puts up her hand.

'What's your name?'

'Sophie.'

'Have you looked after kids before?

She shakes her head.

'No, but I've got loads of cousins. She'll be ok with me for a while.'

'Anybody know her name?'

'Tilly,' someone calls. It strikes me that I should have known these kids' names before today. I hadn't bothered to get to know anyone, really. Didn't think we'd be staying long.

'Right, you sort out Tilly. Is that ok? Does she have siblings?'

Some little kids shake their heads.

'And the one-year-old?'

Standing beside Sophie is a boy, of a similar age.

'What's your name?' I ask him.

'I'm Josh,' says her friend.

'Do you think you can have the two babies together?'

They both shrug and look at each other.

'I'll take that as a yes. You'll be fine, I'll tell you what you need to know. I had a baby sister.'

They look embarrassed. Maybe they know about my sister.

I had a sister. I had a mum. Do I still? I'm not sure. I had a dad. Do I still? I don't know.

'Now then,' I say, standing up to address the group. 'Are there any other children who are missing? Anyone else who lives on the holiday park who isn't here?'

They all look around at each other and try to rack their brains.

'I think that's everyone,' says Josh, looking around, not fully sure of himself.

'Ok. If you're seven or younger, stay here on the rug. If you're eight or older, go to your caravan, get whatever food you can find and bring it back here,' I say.

The kids scarper.

And then they come, in their dressing gowns and slippers, bringing loaves of bread and jars of peanut butter, and jam. They bring plates and cups, milk and knives, and we all have a picnic on the duvets.

By lunchtime, it's carnage. I can't keep tabs on all the children; they keep wandering off. Just because I'm the eldest on the caravan park, everyone assumes I know what I'm doing. Leader by default.

Sophie suggests putting them in groups, with the older kids in charge. Older is a relative term, but it's a good plan.

I stand up and holler. 'Everyone back here!'

A few come but the others ignore me. There is a frenzied football match taking place, and gaggles of children everywhere. A group of boys are poking a lifeless bird with a stick.

I run to the back of our caravan, drag out a piece of corrugated iron we used as a makeshift lid for the shed, and hit it with a hammer.

'Meeting!' I yell. The clanging gets their attention at least and once they're all back on the green, I say, 'Hands up if you're over ten!'

A bunch of hands go up.

'You are now the adults,' I say, trying to sound bright. 'You are responsible for the under-fives that I am assigning to you. You are families, for the time being. You sleep in the same caravan together, you share food together, you stay together, all the time. Do you understand?'

They nod.

I split the little ones up, so they have one or two 'parents' each. The older kids help, by shepherding them all into their families, making sure they have everything they need, except, of course, their actual parents. I assign all the older kids to families too but it's the two-year-olds I'm most worried about. I know what Zozo was like. I remember the time she wandered off into the amusements, and we lost her in the crowd, in amongst the clatter of 2p machines, the beeps and cheesy pop music blaring out over our cries. Mum and Dad had been arguing about whether we could afford fish and chips for supper, and I was looking the other way, as usual. They thought I had her, I thought they had her. We looked down and she was gone.

We found her after five minutes, wandering around the maze of slot machines, staring up at the bright lights. I still remember the feeling of relief that flooded my body when we saw her again, and how good it felt to hug her close to me. I breathed her in like oxygen, swore I'd never let her out of my sight again.

How am I going to keep all these kids safe? It doesn't seem possible.

Just then I notice a girl over at the back of the caravan park, fine hair, down to her waist, sandy colour. Helping where she can, moving between the kids. I hadn't noticed her on the park before. She moves with assurance and calm, looks like she knows exactly what the kids need. She doesn't seem as stressed as everyone else.

'Right guys,' I say to anyone still listening. 'I am going to try to figure out what is going on here. Robin has suggested we all meet at Leysdown playground at five.'

The kids gaze vacantly at me.

'So, you've got a few hours to kill.'

'What are we supposed to do?' someone asks.

'Play tag? Think of it like a long holiday?'

There are a few smiles exchanged at the thought of that. No school.

'And another thing. Don't touch the birds. They have some disease or something.'

Some children don't move from the mat. They don't know where to go. Some go to sleep in their beds or play in their caravans. Some wander around outside. The older kids try to be good, I can tell, hanging around the little ones to make sure they're ok.

I go back to my caravan and pull my phone out to call Robin. *Oh yeah, no network.* I google *Where are the adults?* and then *social services, Sheppey* but each time, a little dial pops up on the screen followed by *INTERNET UNAVAIL-ABLE*. I google *help* knowing it won't work but I type it in anyway. I try to ring 999 again. No service. I miss Robin. Why are we waiting until five to meet? It's hours away.

I get out a pad of paper and start to write.

Where are all the adults? I write, at the top of the page. And then underneath, a list of ideas.

-They have all been arrested (highly unlikely)

-They have all died from some illness and have been taken away in the night while we all slept (impossible)

-They have all disappeared (impossible)

-They have all run away from us – like Mum (highly unlikely)

-The government are using our island as a test centre for something which has gone very badly wrong? (No idea).

-Further to this idea: The adults have been decimated by some heat ray that disintegrated their bodies (hopefully impossible).

-They have been beamed up by aliens. (??!!)

-A slow nuclear bomb has gone off. It has killed the adults and we're next. In fact, the radiation is already eating us alive.

I look down at my hands. They look normal.

It's deeply unsatisfying trawling through all these ideas that are impossible. Literally impossible.

'So, what do I need to do?' I say aloud. I write that down on the paper too, hoping it will give me clarity and a sense of purpose. I write another list.

-Find all the babies.

-Find food – steal what we can.

-Go to the police station.

-Find out what the hell is going on.

-GET OFF THE ISLAND.

I throw my pen down on the table and sigh.

'Dad, what the hell? How could you leave me in this mess? How could you leave just like Mum did?'

There's no answer, obviously.

26

JAY

Saturday 25th September 2021

THERE ARE STILL a few hours before I meet Rob, so I go and knock on the door of my second-in-command: Ronnie, a fourteen-year-old who lives a couple of caravans down.

He's alone, gaming. I walk over to the TV, pull out the cable, and say, 'You're in charge.'

'What?' he says, his hands raised in protest. 'Chill, Jay.'

'No, Ronnie. Life, as you knew it ... Yesterday. That's done man, it's over. You ain't that Ronnie anymore, mate. Come on. Wake up.'

He glares at me, but he gets it.

I cycle to the nearest police station, which is in Sheerness, three quarters of an hour away. There's not a single car on the road. There are a few abandoned though. One that looks like it was run off the road on the way out of Leysdown. An old burgundy Volvo, straight out of the 70s. Nose down in the ditch. I go over for a closer look but it's empty. Well, apart from the clothes – strapped into the two front seats by the belts. It's as if the owners were beamed up by aliens and I wonder if I should amend that entry on the list to 'possible'.

I check some of the other cars too, the ones stopped dead in the middle of the road. Clothes inside the seatbelts, same as the first.

And the birds; they're everywhere, dotted all around the roads. They've smashed themselves to death on the tarmac all over the place. They're all the same: iridescent black feathers like an oil slick, curled claws, lifeless eyes. Starlings.

The police station is small – just an office with living quarters out the back.

I try the door but it's locked. I didn't think they were ever supposed to be locked. I can see a light on inside. I drop my bike to the ground and pull a wheelie bin over to the door. I clamber onto it, using my forearms to pull myself up so I can see through the glass. There's a desk ... that's where the light is coming from, the lamp is still on, and some papers and a pen on the desk. The chair is pushed back. A uniform is draped on the chair.

'Shit' I whisper.

I walk down the side alley, which leads to the attached house. I assume it's where the station house officer lives. I pick up a garden chair and smash it into the glass on the back door. It crumples and gives way.

'HELLO?' I shout into the house.

There's nothing for a moment, but then I hear the whimpering of hungry kids. Reaching in past the broken glass I unlock the door and run upstairs to find two boys, one about a year old, the other maybe three, sitting in the cot together. The older one must have sensed something was wrong and climbed in with the baby. Thankfully they were locked in. *How many more are there?* In my mind, I can see rooms and rooms of kids. I can hear them crying and the anxiety sets my heart racing.

'We must hurry,' I mutter.

'Hi boys, are you ok?' I try to sound cheerful and friendly at the same time.

They cry a little because they don't know me, but also maybe with relief that someone has come for them.

I lift the three-year-old out of the cot and put him on the floor.

'What's your name?'

'Samir,' he says, sniffling.

'Can you show me where your mum sleeps?' I ask, while lifting out the second little boy and holding him.

He nods and shuffles across the hallway.

'Mum gone,' he whispers.

The bed is empty and the clothes laid out in the way she would have been sleeping. I feel chills along my spine again. It's the same all over.

I take a photo for someone. I'm not sure who.

Now what? It's a forty-minute bike ride back to the caravan park and now I've got two kids to carry. I carry the little boy down the stairs and Samir follows us. I give them a drink and some Weetabix. They are happy for the food and eat it noisily while I sit there watching them. It suddenly dawns on me again that life as we know it has ended.

I mean, I hated life as I knew it so that was no bad thing, but all of these kids are shafted. All their parents gone. How can it be true?

'There has to be an explanation.' Samir looks at me, quizzically, not understanding that I'm talking to no one.

When they've finished eating, we walk back out to the

deserted street. Still not a soul in any direction. We walk up the middle of the road, calling out, 'HELLO! ANYONE HERE? ANYONE?' but the only answer is the echo of my own voice.

Birds are scattered on the ground outside the windows of the houses. Looks like they had been trying to get in. Their feathers are ruffled and tatty as if they've been in a fight. I bend down to get a closer look at one, and the bird's lifeless eye looks as though it's still watching me. I nudge it gently with my toe and its claw curls slowly.

I jump and step backwards. It's still alive! I look him in the eye again.

'How could you do this to us?' I whisper. 'Where have you taken them? Where's my dad?'

The starling lies there like a broken doll. So weak in itself, but, when it was part of the body, it was immense. I had seen it for myself.

Why am I blaming the starlings? Have I gone insane?

I keep thinking back to the day before. What was different? It was just a Friday in September.

It was the starlings, that was the only thing, the cloud of them, over the boat, passing over the island, and now, these bird bodies, all over the place.

I'm sure it's too early in the year for them. Didn't Elsie say they normally come in October and November, and didn't they normally roost at four or five, as dusk fell? Why were they here in September and why were they flying over us at the lake late at night? And what about Elsie the other night, crying out for them to take her?

Were they trying to tell us something last night? Was it a warning?

I can't leave the boys but have to get back to my patch. There will be more kids, in each of these buildings, but I haven't got the heart to find them because I know I can't help them all. The thought of their unheard screams churns in my gut.

I breathe out slowly.

'We'll do our best,' I say to the boys. 'And that will have to be enough.'

They nod along.

I go back into the policeman's house, looking for some way to transport the baby and there by the back door is a baby sling. My Mum used one with Zoe. I strap it on and manage to get the baby in place.

'What is your little brother called, Samir?' I ask.

'Raz.'

'I like that name. Right, Samir and Raz, we're just going to get you to a safe place where you can make lots of new friends, ok?'

I put my hand to the door handle and then turn and scribble a note on the back of a gas bill on the kitchen counter. Just in case this is all a mistake. *I've got Raz and Samir. We're at Leysdown Holiday Park. Jay.* I read it back and think it sounds a bit threatening. Oh well, they'll get the message.

I set off with my load, back to Leysdown, having added two problems to my list: it looks like there are no adults on the island at all, and now I had two more children to deal with. I hold Samir in place between my legs on the frame of the bike. I tell the kids to hold on tight and it works for a mile or so, but the stress of dropping either of the boys makes me sweat so we end up walking from about halfway back. I put Samir on the seat of the bike and push him along. At least he doesn't have to walk. The main roads are empty anyway. We stop at Robin's house and find him, standing outside, in the middle of a mass playgroup looking around him frantically. He has one hand on his hip and the other is shading his brow from the sun as he looks for someone. He sees me and starts to walk.

'What are we going to do?' he says, looking at me, helplessly.

'Getting the hell off this island would be a good start,' I reply, taking Samir down from the bike. Raz has fallen asleep in the sling.

'In seriousness, I have no idea.'

A baby is screaming, and a girl is walking in circles with it, jigging it on her hip.

'Do you know where this baby lives?' I ask her.

She gestures to the house opposite with her chin.

'Can you show me?' I ask.

She nods and we cross over the road, Samir following.

I raid the cupboards until I find what I'm looking for: a clean bottle, a box of formula. I haven't done it for a while, but I used to make up feeds for Zoe and it was easy enough. You just have to boil water to rinse out the bottle, then five scoops of powder, five ounces of water. Let it cool. Easy.

'There we go, that should fill him up a bit,' I say. 'Is there another bottle? Raz will probably want one when he wakes up.'

She points vaguely to the cupboard while jiggling the squirming baby on her non-existent hips.

The crying baby wakes Raz who starts crying when he sees the bottle.

'Yes, yes, yes, I'll get one for you,' I say, wondering how Mum ever got anything done when Zozo was little.

'You make sure you wait until it's cooled down a bit. Splash some on your wrist and when its warm not hot, it'll be fine for him.'

She nods.

'See it says here how many feeds he needs a day, too.'

She nods again, with tears in her eyes.

'I know it's a lot,' I say, wondering where this grown-up inside me has emerged from. 'But Robin's here to help you,' I say.

She nods again and wipes her eyes.

'It'll only be for a day or so, until we figure out what's going on, ok? It's scary, I know. But we'll figure it out.'

I make a bottle for Raz and take it back out to the patch of green in between the houses. We sit in a circle: me, Samir and Raz, Rob, Ava, the girl and the baby. Some of the other kids copy us and sit down too, bringing white bread and water for Samir.

'Well, the police are gone,' I say to Robin. 'Next thing is to make sure we can keep ourselves going with food.'

'Don't you just wonder what has happened?' says Robin. 'How can you think about food?'

'Of course I do! I have no idea what's happened! All I know is it's big. Didn't see a single adult just now. But we have to stay alive until we find out.'

'Have you seen Swanny again?'

Robin shakes his head.

'Mate, we'll figure it out,' I say, looking at him. 'We'll get off the island. We'll find someone to help.'

But as I say it, his chin trembles, and he draws his knees up to his chest.

'I don't know, Jay. It feels like it's the end of the world.'

'I know it does, but it can't be because we're still here.'

He nods and sniffs his tears away.

'Listen, do you think you can find some people to take care of these two? I need to get back to the caravan park.'

Robin laughs, wipes his eyes, and says, 'Yes, we'll sort something out.'

I go to hug him. I aim for a slap-on-the-back man-hug, but he pulls me in, and his fingers clutch me tight.

'It *will* be ok,' I say, holding his arms and looking into his red-rimmed eyes, not believing a word of it.

As I WHEEL my bike away, I turn, and look back at them sitting there on the grass, knowing that I have given Robin more than he can cope with. But what else can I do? I've got to get back.

'See you at five,' I call over my shoulder.

27

JAY

Saturday 25th September 2021

THE KIDS COME out of their hiding places by five on the first day. Even if they are terrified, the hunger draws them. They come to Leysdown playground, even if they haven't been told about the meeting. It's the only place the little ones know how to get to. The word spreads to those who haven't already heard, and to those who are scared. They file into the mud arena, the flat area between the slide and the parched maze of conifer trees. Looking out, I can see the older kids, their eyes wide with stress and fear, trying to keep a hold of the little ones, who want to run around their legs, or go and play hide and seek. They are all hungry by now. Swanny has finally emerged.

'We are an island all to ourselves!' he cries, standing in the middle of his stunned audience. 'No parents. They've gone! We can do whatever the hell we like!' He spins around, his arms outstretched.

His deranged screeching bounces off the dry earth. He lets out a whoop, which falls flatly amongst the whimpering and hush of the still shell-shocked kids. No one else is excited.

Swanny is hungry, demented, high, his eyes ranging around him like a wild dog.

I walk up to him, pat him on the shoulder, and say, 'Mate, we need to work together. These kids are scared out of their minds.'

Swanny jumps a mile when I touch him. His body isn't used to it.

'Are you ok?' I say, looking him in the eyes. His pupils are dilated and suddenly I see his Achilles, just like he had seen mine on the boat last night. He's as scared as the rest of us. All of this performance is just a facade. I don't break the illusion, I let him continue with his act, but he knows that I know.

And last night, on the boat – it's already a million years ago. Everything is different.

A voice emerges, and to my surprise, it's mine. Mine is the voice of reason that the children need.

'Listen up everyone. We need to talk about what happened. We can figure this out together, we can look after each other.'

My voice is the steadying balm that calls out like a beacon across Leysdown playground and comes up with a plan. I don't know why it's me, but the voice comes out before I can protest. The need comes before the fear. No one challenges me. I'm only seventeen but my world has fallen apart once already, and I lived through it. And nothing could be worse than what I've already faced. Even this.

'Let's start with last night. Does anyone know what happened? Did anyone see anything?'

Then they all start to talk, all on top of each other, a cacophony of noise.

'A dark cloud.'

'Fluttering and wind.'

'A storm, it woke me up and I went into Mum and Dad, and they weren't there anymore,' says a little girl, her face crumpling as she talks.

I wonder why I didn't wake in the night, even with the booze. How could I have slept through something like this?

'Ok. Our first job is to make sure everyone has a foster family. We need to make sure no one is missing. We need to find out how many babies there are, and make sure they are cared for like we've done on the Leysdown Holiday park. Is everyone accounted for? Have a think. Are there any children who you haven't seen today?' I ask, and then they all look around at each other and start to vaguely shake their heads.

'Ok, so we think everyone is here. Next, we need to get food. We need to know how far this has spread and what is happening. We need to get word to the mainland.'

The children start to nod, and their tears stop a little.

'We need tools. We're going to have to loot the local shops at least until tomorrow. But we need to be fair. No hoarding. We're in this together. We share everything we find, ok? Even Swanny is listening now. Out the corner of my eye I can see him nodding. There's the Sunny Convenience store, the farm shop at Brambledown, the Spar at Leysdown. That's our nearest three. And after that, we need to get the hell off the island. Does anyone have any questions?'

I look out to a sea of blank faces.

'Rob, Ronnie, and everyone else who is fifteen or older, I want you to go and get all the food you can and bring it back to the caravan park.'

They nod back at me and start to gather over to one side.

I scan the crowd of children and there's that girl again, at the back. Just the sight of her stops me in my thought trail and makes me forget what I am saying. She looks up at the pause in my speech and sees me staring right at her. She smiles a little.

'Erm ...' I stumble. 'So we'll start off with the Spar. You guys take a trolley, bring it all back to the caravan park. We'll settle there tonight, and tomorrow we're going to have to try to get off the island. We just need enough food for a night. Something to eat now and something for breakfast. I'm sure someone will come for us in the morning, word must have got out by now.' But even as I am speaking, a tremor in my voice belies all of my words. They would have come by now. If there was anyone to come, they would have come. I can't work out if I'm talking myself into or out of fear. Word must have reached the mainland by now, so why isn't anyone coming to help us? The Swale is only a mile wide. So why is it taking them so long to reach us? Surely they know something is up? Even if our phones are out on this side, someone must have been able to walk over the bridge?

And what if they're all gone too? What if there is no one to come and help? I can't worry about that yet, though. One thing at a time. Eat and then sleep.

And then I see him in the background, a white smudge behind the conifer maze. A brown hazelnut of an eye, a dirty white vest. It's him. Kit from the caravan park. We had forgotten him.

And then I think again of all the other forgotten ones, the ones we don't know. They will die if we don't find them.

I won't be able to sleep until we knock on every door, go to every flat, find every child.

I send ten of the older kids off on their bikes as runners to search as many houses as they can. Swanny leads the group as they pedal off into the dusk. I tell them to make a list of the streets they cover so we know we haven't missed anywhere.

There's so much ground to cover, but we have to try. For every kid who goes out, I say to them, if there's not enough people to look after them where they are, bring them back to the caravan park. We'll keep going tomorrow and for as long as it takes. Spread the word. I feel bad sending them off as the light is falling, but the urgency has just hit me again. We have to get them out now, the youngest ones might not last the night.

I watch the kids huddle after I finish talking. The older kids pick up the babies, the little boys tussle, the teenagers walk about with terror in their eyes. I can feel my strength melt away. The kids seem convinced that I know what I'm doing, when really, I don't have a clue, I'm just blagging it.

If I hadn't found Samir and Raz earlier on I would have cycled out to the bridge, to see if I could see the mainland, to see if there were cars moving, signs of industry, or people. We haven't seen any planes go over in the last day, but there are hardly any at the moment anyway. I want to go up to Sheppey port too, to see if there's anybody there. There must be ships coming in all the time. Even though I couldn't get far, the scene on the road had told me that whatever happened was widespread; I didn't see a single adult on my way there or back.

I need to find out if it's just us, some random island thing, or if it has happened in the UK too, or even the whole world. What if it is the end of the world and we've been forgotten in some cosmic blip? What if we're the only ones left?

The kids start to dissipate, the girls walk off in huddles, and even the boys are a little more subdued now. It is 6.30pm and the day starts to fade to pink.

A few kids come up to give me high fives or ask me questions that I can't answer.

'I'll knock on your doors later to see you're ok,' I say. 'If anyone needs anything, I'm number three, at the top of the park.'

I feel a heaviness, a dog-tiredness, seeping into my bones. I sit down where I am, on top of the mound, and the enormity of everything creeps up on me. I realise that I haven't eaten anything all day. We have to keep the kids safe, that's all that matters. After what happened to Zozo, I can't let anything happen to any of these kids.

But we're not enough – we don't know how to look after babies. We don't know first aid. How can we cover the whole of this island on our bikes, breaking into houses, not knowing what we might find? We're wading into adult life in a flash, on a crazy whim, and I sure as anything ain't ready for it.

What next? I think, as I sit there.

I reach into my pocket for a ciggie, the second of the day. It calms my nerves a little.

I watch the girl walking around, helping where she can. She seems to be becoming the mum that all the kids need; they all swarm to her for cuddles and games. And she seems to take it in her stride, a natural.

It's as if I've sidestepped into a different world – one where birds have the power to disintegrate adults and beautiful people turn up out of nowhere. She's definitely not from the island; I would remember if I'd seen her before.

I see the little vest running past me again, a blur in the dusk. He leaps over a bush, and darts behind a wall. There is something about the way he runs, turning and jumping like a nymph, something about the way he crooks his elbow behind him as he runs, an exaggerated race start position that makes me want to hold him and never let him go. He runs just like Zoe did.

He keeps putting himself in my eyeline, making me notice him. He needs my help. Last time, I ignored him and carried on with my own life.

'Hey Kit,' I call, running over to him. 'Stop!'

I kneel and hug him tight. He doesn't move, like he feels shocked to be held. His bones are rigid, his frame is as small as a bird's. He is cold.

'Has your grown up gone, Kit?' I ask.

He nods and stares at me defiantly.

'They all have, don't worry. Do you have a family of kids?'

He shakes his head.

'Do you want to stay with me now?'

He nods.

More than the others, he needs someone. I can see a thirsty look in his eyes, a look of longing. For food, warmth, safety. For love.

'Do you need some food?'

He nods, hungrily, needily.

'Me too.'

I can see Kit is tired. He's been on survival mode for way longer than any of us, and he knows that he needs to be looked after now. I pick him up like I used to pick Zozo up, and he curls himself around me, his legs around my hips, his arms around my neck, his face buried in my chest.

He doesn't care that he barely knows me, he just knows

he's tired and needs taking care of. His skin is cold and covered with goosebumps. I ache for Zoe with a cavernous longing.

As I carry him, he whispers in my ear, 'There was a nurse who was meant to come but then she stopped coming. I've ran out of money now. Aunty Jenny didn't have any left. And now she's gone too. But I was meant to look after her. She couldn't get up, she hadn't for a long time.'

'All the grown-ups have gone. You haven't done anything wrong. You did the best you could, Kit,' I say, not knowing anything of what he's had to do.

'Is it my fault she's gone?'

'No, Kit, all the adults have gone.'

He buries his head into my shoulder.

'It's ok,' I say. 'I'm not going anywhere.'

As I say it, I wonder if it's true. Who knows what the future holds now? But I do know what it's like to be left behind, and now all these kids do too.

When we get back to the caravan park, I say to Kit, 'Shall we just grab you some clothes?'

Kit shrugs and looks down at his feet.

His caravan stinks of sweat and mildew. I can't bear to be inside for any longer than I have to. I glance over at the bedroom, see the door ajar, the sheets scrunched up. I put my head out of the door and take a deep breath of fresh air and then step back inside the bedroom. Clothes laid out, same as the others. I don't need to stay any longer.

Out on the step again, I look Kit in the eye and say, 'Is there anything you want to bring with you?'

Kit shakes his head, staring at the concrete slab he's standing on.

'Where are your clothes kept?'

Kit shrugs. 'There aren't none,' he says.

I frown. 'There must be something.' But as I say it, I realise I've seen him several times and he's always been wearing the same thing – that grubby white vest and joggers.

I take another deep breath and dive back into the musty air of the bedroom. Clothes litter the floor, the stench of unmade beds, sweat, a blocked toilet, and rotting food is unbearable.

I bend to pick up a few bits of clothing, and then change my mind.

'Do you know what, Kit? We'll find you something else.'

Why would he want to remember anything of this life? We close the door for good on that caravan.

THE SKY SETTLES INTO INDIGO, and the chill deepens around the caravan park.

I knock on the door of the caravan two doors down, now occupied by a new family of kids.

'Hey guys,' I say. 'This is Kit. He needs some clothes. Do you have any you can give him? Age five-ish?'

'I'm seven,' Kit says quietly.

'Oh, sorry. Age seven then.'

There are six kids inside: Sophie and Josh, a younger boy and girl, the baby and the one-year-old. They bring out a couple of t-shirts, some joggers, and a dressing gown.

'That's great. Have you got any pants and socks? And a hoodie? And a coat?'

They scurry away to find them.

'Sorry Will, this is all your old stuff,' Will's younger sister says. 'You don't mind though, do you? You've got loads.'

Will shrugs, and as I turn to leave he says quietly, 'Do you think they're coming back?'

'I don't know. I hope so. I just ... it's just ... nothing like this has ever happened before. We'll find out what happened, don't worry. Just keep safe for tonight, ok?'

He nods and they all stand there staring at me as if I know something they don't. Seven hungry faces. Hungry for answers. Answers that I don't have.

Will speaks again.

'It's just that. Well, what if there's something out there?'

'Hmm.'

I open my mouth to speak and realise that I haven't even thought of that possibility.

'I don't really think an animal or whatever could have done this,' I say, but there's no way to rationalise what was likely or unlikely. The whole thing was impossible, but it had happened. Whatever it was.

'I'll find out,' I say, hating that I was sounding more and more like a politician by the second. Spouting the thing they want to hear and hoping they'll be happy enough. That was what they thought, and I was falling into the trap myself. 'Just lock your doors tonight, and we'll see what tomorrow brings, hey?'

'Mum and Dad always locked the door, and it still got them.'

'I know. I'm sorry. Just try to get some rest. Try to think about something else, hey?'

'What like?'

'Erm. Maybe you could have a game of *I spy* or tell some jokes?'

Will looks unconvinced.

I feel like a fraud as I feed him my lines. But there's nothing else I can offer him. No reassurance. There is no explanation, and as far as we know, it could happen again.

We walk back across the green to our caravan and I turn

and see Swanny raging across the field. I wonder why he's back so soon – he's meant to be searching for kids.

'Oi Swan, you alright?' I call over the field.

He juts his chin up by way of a greeting and strides towards me. He doesn't slow down until he is right in my face, pushing his face into mine.

'I never signed up for this, Jay,' he spits.

'Mate, none of us did.'

He pulls back, his eyes gleaming. I don't ask him what he found.

'I ain't going baby hunting no more. I can't deal with it.'

'Don't worry mate, just do what you can. We'll find someone else to do it. You're good with food though, right? You can gather food for us?'

He nods. 'Yeah, yeah, I can do food.' And turns and marches away.

BACK AT THE CARAVAN, I run a shower for Kit and help him to wash. I can see the outline of ribs through his skin. His bony shoulder blades jut out, his skin is oily with grime. I watch the dirt running down the plughole and feel so sad for him, that he's been surviving like this for so long. I lived so close to him and had no idea. I don't ask him any more questions; he'll talk when he's ready.

After the shower, Kit changes into a clean t-shirt, joggers and a dressing gown.

'We forgot to ask to borrow pyjamas, didn't we? Never mind. I'm pretty sure we have a Simpsons DVD – do you like that?' I ask. Kit shrugs. 'And you must be hungry. Want some toast?'

He nods. I get him a piece of toast and jam and watch him eat it, greedily.

The TV has stopped working. We tried to get the news earlier, but we could only find blank channels, so it was DVDs or nothing.

Watching him eat, I think about how temporary everything is. How all of our past lives have just shrivelled up into a ball. All the parents gone. Sucked up? Disintegrated? Held hostage? Where are they? It feels like we're spiralling into death somehow, being sucked down into a state of non-being. Feels like we're stuck in a cosmic glitch, like someone had pulled the rug from under us but it had got stuck halfway, like the end of the world was coming, but had just stopped short. That's Sheppey for you.

'I'm just going to make up a bed for you, ok?'

He has finished eating and is now blissfully absorbed in the Simpsons. He nods, distractedly.

I go into Dad's room to make up the bed for Kit, but going in and closing the door, I stop. I haven't had time to think about the fact that Dad is missing. I've been too busy figuring out what to do with all the kids. That's both halves of me lost now: Mum and Dad. Rob already took a photo of the room, but I can't bring myself to strip the bed. It's a crime scene after all, the last known place of a loved one. And then I realise, everything is just as Dad had left it, and if I move anything, I'll have nothing left of Dad, until he comes back. If he comes back.

And then I don't want to touch a single thing.

I breathe in deeply and try to store the scent deep in my brain. Dad feels so near. I sit on the edge of the bed, the white duvet cover still pulled back from this morning, when Robin and I came in.

I look at the vest and boxers that Dad wore to bed last night and I press my flat palm to them.

I turn to go and make my bed up for Kit instead but

notice a photo of Mum tucked behind one corner of the mirror and a picture of Zozo tucked behind the other corner. I miss them so much. I sit there for a minute, looking at their faces, the quiet ringing in my ears. And then I see Mum's diary on the shelf. *Why is that here?*

When we moved, we just picked the things we liked the best out of the old house. There was way more stuff than we could fit into the caravan. We had a car boot sale for the rest. Made a hundred quid. It was the first time we had been through Mum and Zoe's stuff. I picked a few bits out for me. Dad kept the photos, but they made me too sad. Figured I'd rather carry them in my heart. I found a diary of Mums, asked if I could keep it. Dad said sure. I didn't know what I'd take to remember Zozo. Then I saw one of her hair clips, with a little unicorn on it. I shoved the notebook and the clip into my rucksack and then carried on loading and sorting.

All the rest of it was just stuff, wasn't it? It wasn't them. We hadn't even been into Zoe's bedroom since the day Mum went. It was too painful, so we just shut the door on it.

But then the first night in the caravan, I looked through Mum's diary. There were tear-stained rambles about Zoe, rants about Dad, and then, on the last page, a couple of poems.

I pick it up again and try her words out on my tongue, letting them inhabit my body again, willing it all to fall into place, to switch a light on, to show me something I've never seen before.

Sometimes it is the weight that you take in a place.
Or not.
Sometimes you feel as if no one would even notice if you were gone.
Sometimes you feel as if you were a bird, a tiny skeleton,

*and that it would be just as well to go and land somewhere
else.*
When all you really want is for someone to look at you,
to look at the space where you were,
to say, something has gone from here,
something has taken flight.

I WANT to answer her back, say: 'Mum, we did see you! We loved you! We needed you!' but it's too late for any of that.

Perhaps Mum did want to go. It gives me no satisfaction to see it written there in black and white.

Right now, sitting in Dad's bedroom, I have a feeling of walking away from all of this. Everything is going to be different from now on. But who am I without Mum, Dad and Zozo?

I don't change the bed. Instead, I put down the diary, carefully close the door, and shut time in a box, just as me and Dad did before.

I wait there for a moment, my hand on the door handle, saying something. What? A prayer? I don't pray. Goodbye, perhaps?

I go into my room, tidy it quickly, and put fresh sheets on the bed. When I come back through to the lounge, Kit has already fallen asleep with the Simpsons still blaring out. I pick him up, light as anything, carry him through to the bedroom and tuck him in. I wonder when the last time was that he was warm. I wonder how he used to put himself to bed with a bedridden aunty that he was supposed to be looking after. I wonder how he looked after her, whether he talked to her, what he had to do for her. I can't believe he's been carrying all of that on his skinny shoulders.

· · ·

LATER ON THAT NIGHT, there is a tap on the door.

It's the girl.

'Hi,' she says, almost in a whisper.

There's something about her that makes me think she isn't quite there, like she could disappear at any moment.

'You ok?' I ask.

She nods.

'I thought I'd say hi.'

'Where did you come from?' I say. 'I've never seen you before.'

'I could see you needed help.'

'The kids seem to like you.'

She smiles, and looks at me strangely, her head cocked slightly to one side, as if she's waiting for something.

I'm not sure what.

'Do you want something? Food, a drink? Have you got somewhere to stay?'

'I'm fine,' she says, that half-smile playing on her lips. 'I'll see you tomorrow.'

She turns and vanishes into the darkness.

I suddenly remember that I said I'd check the kids were ok, tucked in, safe for the night. I'd forgotten to go and now I didn't want to leave Kit.

'Hey,' I call out. 'Are you still there?'

There's no answer, just the far-off crashing of the tide on the shore. She hadn't even told me her name.

I stand at the doorway of the caravan, listening to the waves crash onto the beach. It could have been any of the hundred or so days of this last year, as we clung to the edge of the world in our tinny caravan. Any of them, unchanging. But it's this one, the strangest one, the birds one, the missing parents one. The day when everything changed.

Part of me wants to get out of here, get in a boat, or swim

to the mainland. What will I do when I get there, though? Who knows if there are any adults left alive? And also, how can I swim, how can I steal a boat when I'm scared to death of the black water that stole Mum and all of her dreams away?

I couldn't leave the kids anyway, none of this is their fault. I know what it's like to lose everything. I know what it's like to be left behind.

If I'm only as strong as the weakest among us, then I am a helpless baby. We do this together or we die trying. Fear stops me in my tracks in each direction. Fear of death. Fear of drowning. Fear of being abandoned. I'll stay with the kids, there's no other option.

Part of me wonders if everything will be back to normal when I wake the next day; if all of this is just a product of the dodgy beer that Swanny plied me with last night.

I fall asleep wishing with my whole being that life will just go back to the way it was before, even though I hated it so much.

Anything is better than this.

I WAKE in the night with a start. Dreaming of Mum. In my dreams, she is always leaving. There are so many different dreams, but they all end the same way.

It's night and Dad and I are asleep. In my dream I watch Mum as she takes one last look at me sleeping and then she wraps her arms around her own broken heart and walks away, carrying it with her like a smashed pot.

She is wearing a black leather jacket. She looks at me over her shoulder, blows me a kiss and runs away.

We are underwater and she makes the signal for ok, her thumb and forefinger pressed together, blows a mouthful of bubbles into my face, and turns and swims into the murky depths. I squint my eyes to look for her, but she fades into the darkness.

I am listening to her voice down the telephone line. She says, 'Jay, you misunderstood. I had no choice. I love you; you know that' and I am struggling to talk, struggling to breathe. I have all these arguments that come up to the surface, but when I try to talk, no sound comes out, and I can't make her stay.

She is laughing at me, covering her mouth, and creasing up into a ball. That's the worst one.

I dream about her all the time. I hate her and I love her, and it is all rolled into one. Sometimes I can't even remember her face. There are photos, of course, well there were. Dad only kept a few.

Sometimes I'm searching for her face and it terrifies me. It's like I'm scrabbling at soil, trying to find some image of her that is robust and true, that won't fade, but all I come up with is handfuls of mud, and then sometimes, I don't even know what is real anymore.

I try to imagine how she would look now if she were still alive. I wonder if I would even know her in a crowd.

Mum. Mama. Mummy.

First word from my lips. Biggest question in my life.

My heart thunders.

I lie there, in the dark, waiting for the morning. Wondering what Mum has got to do with any of this.

28

———

FEE

S aturday 25th September 2021

HE IS strange and lovely this boy.
When he looks at me,
it is as though he looks through me and towards another place.
It is like he has always known me.
I can tell that I unnerve him.
He knows I am untethered
where he is tied down.
It doesn't feel like he is from the island, somehow.
this strange place; so small, such big skies.
He is different to the others.

I AM COMING, Papa.
This is the way; I can feel it in my bones.

I will find you, come hell or high water.
Hell has already come, and the high water is coming next.

I⊤ DOESN'T FEEL *time to leave yet, though.*
    And I can't go on my own; even I am not that stupid.
    But who can I ask? The boy? His sidekick?
    He doesn't love me enough to risk his life for me. Not yet.

29

JAY

Sunday 26th September 2021

I WAKE in my makeshift bed on the sofa to the scrape of a can being kicked along the tarmac.

My eyes flick open. I remember.

My arms are curved around Kit's legs, who is at rest at last. I wonder when the last time was that he slept well.

He woke, crying in the night, and I let him top and tail next to me, the way Zozo used to sometimes. He fell back to sleep in the end, twitching and fidgeting until the warmth of the bed lulled him asleep.

He reminds me so much of Zozo.

It burns under my skin like anger that she isn't here now.

Mum was wildly in love with Zoe before she'd even met her. As soon as she found out Zoe was coming she developed a glow about her, a reason for living. I love remembering how much Mum loved her. Me too, I suppose.

She was so wanted, that little girl, so loved.

She told me they'd been trying for years after they had me, but it just wasn't happening. I didn't even realise she was sad or missing anything. I was so loud with my own needs.

Dad being Dad, didn't want any intervention. Mum had all the tests, but everything seemed fine.

'You've had one – think yourself lucky,' the doctors said. 'It might happen one day.'

So, she drank less, took multivitamins, ran up the coast, prayed.

And then it did happen.

Twelve years after they had me, they had Zoe.

She was the missing jigsaw piece. Sure, Zoe pulled at Dad's heart strings, but he didn't dream her into being like Mum did. As if by magic.

There's a photo of us, a selfie. Mum had it as the screen saver on her phone. Mum, me and Zozo on the path up to Warden. Wind blowing the hair away from our faces, our eyes crinkling into the wind. Funny when you look back at a photo, a moment in time, a snapshot, and you realise it was everything that you never even knew you wanted.

All together, all happy, and that was all that mattered.

I lie there, my eyes half-awake in the orange glow of the curtains. I push myself up on my elbows and open the curtains a crack. A boy in a yellow hoodie is dribbling a can around as if it is a football.

How can all of this be true? Zozo, Mum and now Dad? How could it only have been a day ago that everything was normal?

Faces flash through my mind: Dad, Pete, Elsie, Aunty

Suz. Have they really all gone? I roll onto my back and look up at the ceiling.

I have to find an adult today. It's just not possible that they've all gone.

There's a knock at the door. I creep out of bed, leaving Kit dozing. It's Rob, white-faced, looking exhausted.

'We found fourteen more,' he says.

'Mate, you look awful. Have you slept? Where's Ava?'

He shakes his head.

'She's with a girl who used to babysit. I went out with the runners. We did as much as we could. There are other groups of kids, huddling in houses. They're all terrified. And no, I haven't slept.'

'But you told them all to keep looking? We can't let any die.'

'I know Jay, we all just need to stay alive. The lads are looking. You have to let it go now; help is going all over the island; we'll find them all eventually. And people know where to come if they need help, I've told the kids to come here if they need anything. Groups are starting up all over the island.'

'Ok sure. Feel like I should go and check the prisons today. There has to be someone there.'

Rob says nothing. He doubts it. His face says it all. He turns to go.

I gently wake Kit, and we have a hurried breakfast of bread and peanut butter, and then I say, 'I need to check all the caravans, to see if everyone's ok. Do you want to come too?'

He nods and follows me. I wonder if I've tamed him, somehow, by looking after him, whether I've taken some of the wildness out of him. He seems younger today, reticent. He doesn't want to leave my side now. But maybe that's what he needed. To not have to survive on his own for once.

We step outside and there's a girl sobbing on the road.

'We've lost one of the kids,' she cries.

'Ok, don't panic,' I say, feeling sick.

We shout for people to come and help to look and comb the caravan site. After twenty minutes or so, we find him crouching in a blackberry bush. These kids don't know how to be parents, do they?

'Just try to keep a closer eye on him, ok?' I say to the girl, not really wanting to tell her off.

She nods, sniffs down her tears, and holds the toddler in her arms.

I leave her and walk up to the gate with Kit, where Old Pete's caravan stood like a sentinel over the park, thinking I'd go systematically around the park. Pete's caravan was part hidden by an old conifer hedge. He wanted to live in the most private one, and since he got here first, he got first dibs. We didn't check it yesterday. There's a nagging insistence inside me that makes me want to check it now, though. We walk over towards it and there's a bird lying on the top step, its feathers shining silkily in the morning light.

I notice a window is slightly ajar, and I use a stick to prise it open. I drag over a plastic chair and push my head up through the gap. I can see a leg outstretched on the lino, poking out from behind the breakfast island.

'Pete!' I cry, and stumble to get off the chair. 'He's in there!'

Without thinking, I grab a stone that was weighing down one of Pete's plastic picnic chairs. I smash it into the door, one, two three, four times. The glass gives way, curves back and in on itself and then shatters onto the floor.

'Pete!' I call out. 'Pete?'

I reach through the smashed glass to undo the latch from the other side and the door swings open. Pete is motionless. I go over to him and kneel alongside him in the galley kitchen. He's breathing, and still warm.

'Pete, are you ok?'

As soon as I touch him, his eyes flick over to me with a smile of recognition.

'Jay,' he mouths.

'Are you ok? What happened?'

Pete shakes his head, mouths, 'The birds, the birds.'

I take his hand and hold it tight. I nod for him to continue.

'What did they do to you?'

'They took my bad heart. They put a new one in, or something. Must have been too rotten to take as I was. I must be dreaming.' He laughs, a sad, wry laugh.

I sit down on the lino next to Pete, my back against the cupboard, and sigh. Kit has followed me into the caravan and tucks himself under my arm. He doesn't look at Pete.

'The birds,' I say quietly, and wonder if there can be any truth in it, or if Pete is hallucinating. He seems close to the end, and we sit with him. I don't panic or try to get help. There isn't any help to get. I hold his hand and feel strangely calm. Two days ago, I never would have imagined this.

His breathing gets shallower and shallower. He isn't scared, or frantic as I thought he might have been. He seems happy to fade away. His checked shirt is undone and I can see a line of pink. I pull open his shirt a little and there's a fresh scar running from the top of his chest down to his navel, as if he's had surgery or something. It's raised and warm to the touch. I don't know if he'd ever had surgery, but certainly not recently. We were in the Black Dog enough to have known if he had.

'Pete, did you have an op?' I whisper.

'No, no,' he mouths, tears in his eyes and a smile on his face. 'It was the birds, like I told you.'

'Kit, why don't you go and find some of the kids? I'll catch up with you in a bit.'

Kit edges to the door and then I see him sprint across the green to join the others through the open doorway.

I stay with Pete until the end. The breaths get fewer and fewer and when I don't hear one for a long time, I just sit there with him.

I've never watched someone die before.

Across the green, I see the girl from last night, sitting, cuddling Tilly while Sophie, her new carer, has a nap. Kit is playing out there too with some of the other boys. I walk towards her.

'Hi.'

The girl looks up at me and her electric-blue eyes flash with something – beauty, mischief? I notice the lightest dusting of freckles over the bridge of her nose. I haven't been this close to her in the light before. And she is as real as anything, but mysterious too.

'I just found an adult. But he's dead now.'

'Oh,' she says quietly. She doesn't seem surprised.

'What's your name? You didn't say last night.'

'Fee,' she says.

'Fee. Can you stay with Kit for a while? Maybe get him some lunch? I need to go to the prison. It's the biggest concentration of life on the island. I need to see if anyone is there.'

She nods. 'Sure. You can stay with me, Kit. We'll be alright, won't we?'

He nods. He trusts her already. So did I, and I didn't

know her at all. There's something about her, something familiar.

Fee smiles a half-smile and then turns back to Kit and the baby.

I can't explain my trust in her. I don't even know her, but in my gut, I know that she should be here, and it almost feels as if she's been sent to help me.

I watch her for a minute before I turn to go. She's full of compassion. An adult already – responsible, level-headed. She looks as light as a feather, as light as a bird. Her skin is pale, and her hair is too. She looks like she comes from the north, Scandinavia or somewhere. She's not from the island, that's for sure. Her ears are so small and thin. Her cheek-bones jut out from her face and make her look, well, older than me. Even her fingers seem barely there.

She's beautiful. But not just beautiful.

Blindingly, heart-stoppingly so.

I cycle down to the prisons. The watch tower is deserted, the gatehouse locked. I take a chance and scale the huge blue fence at the entrance. It is an emergency after all. There's not a sound around the prison. Just the bright blue sky, the clouds sailing across, the gulls calling from far away.

I run across the forecourt and up to the main reception. It's unlocked but deserted. I can't get through to the rest of the prison; it's sealed behind locked doors. I go behind the desk though and look at the monitors flicking between CCTV screens of each cell. On the grainy black and white screens I can make out beds, piles of clothes, but no one there in any of the cells. It's completely empty. There must be a centralised CCTV system though, I think. Someone else must be able to see this. So why is no one coming to help us? I try the phones, but the line is dead.

I set off back to the caravan park and as I turn onto the

main road I pass the lane that runs down to the estuary, and I think of Elsie.

She claimed to know the birds. If anyone knew what was going on, it would be her. If anyone was a friend to the birds, it was her. She has devoted her whole life to them. They wouldn't have taken her too, surely?

I cycle out to her house, but I can tell as I approach that there is no one there. The washing has blown off the line and is scattered on the floor of the yard, and the door is wide open. The wind runs right through the place.

'Elsie?' I call out, anyway. 'Are you there?'

Bernie comes out and starts whining at me.

I step into the cool, dark house and Bernie seems to want me to follow him up the narrow stairs, up to the top bedroom. He climbs a few steps and turns to look at me, then up another few and the same again. I follow him. Up in Elsie's bedroom, there is a small desk in one corner and a single bed in the other. Both windows are open – the curtains flying into the room with the breeze, and there are papers scattered all over the floor. I bend to pick up one of the pages. The title reads *Come Birds, Come*. Did she know they were coming? She said all that stuff about the time running out, didn't she? I gather the papers and shove them into my rucksack.

Bernie is still whining at my feet.

'What is it, you stupid dog?' I say, exasperated.

I turn, and there on the floor behind me is a pile of Elsie's clothes. Her cargo pants and shirt, her moth-eaten sweater and gilet. It gives me goosebumps each time I see one of these sites of disappearance. Bernie takes the gilet in his jaws and offers it to me.

'I'm sorry, buddy, but I don't know where she's gone,' I say, ruffling the fur on his head.

Bernie carries the gilet over to the open window and sits there sadly whining into the air.

'Is that where the trail goes cold, buddy? The window? Is that where she went?' I say, pointing to the open window.

He whines in reply.

I think back to all the open windows, the birds crashed on the ground outside. I peer out of Elsie's window and look down. Sure enough, there are two bird carcasses down there, smashed on the ground below.

'Hey Bernie, do you want to come with me?' I ask.

He growls, which I take as a no. He's a faithful dog, and he won't leave his master even if she has already left him.

'Ok buddy,' I say. 'I've got to go.'

I go down to the kitchen and open Bernie's last three cans of dog food. I empty them into three separate bowls, and line them up on the floor for him. I don't know when or if I'll be back again.

'This is it, Bernie. This is all that's left.'

I put out two bowlfuls of water and crouch down to stroke the back of his neck as he hungrily gobbles at the first bowl of food.

'You're gonna have to fend for yourself now, old boy,' I say, and then add, 'Between you and me, there's a lot of birds out here.'

On the way out of the house, I notice another room off the hallway. I put my head in - it looks like Elsie's study. There is a desk in the corner with a computer on it. I move the mouse to wake up the screen. It shows an internet page, unloaded. The address bar says sceapig.net.

I take out my phone to get a picture of the address. My battery is already down to ten percent. *What did she know and what clues did she leave?*, I wonder, looking around.

30

———

JAY

S unday 26th September 2021

'THE PRISONS ARE EMPTY,' I say breathlessly to Fee when I get back.

As soon as Kit sees me coming, he gets up and stands by my side.

'We have to try to get off the island. Do we try the bridge? All of us, march out there? It's a long walk, though, pushing on three hours.'

'Yes, let's all go,' she says.

'Ok. I'll go round the caravans, tell everyone to pack a rucksack with food and water. We'll leave in half an hour.'

I'm tired beyond reason. I haven't showered since before the lake. I can't sleep, I've hardly eaten. I'm desperate. But we can't just sit around waiting.

I approach the nearest caravan – a circle of kids are gathered and shouts and screams come from inside the circle.

I push my way through to the front to see two girls fighting. One shoves the other away from her with all of her strength, sending her opponent flying back across the circle.

'You bitch – we don't want you in our family!' she screams.

'What the hell?' I shout.

Some of the kids turn to look at me but the fight carries on. I step into the centre of the circle.

'This is not happening!' I shout as loud as I can.

'She stinks – we don't want her!' shouts the girl doing all the pushing and shoving.

The other one openly sobs and crumples to the floor.

'We've lost everything. How can you be so cruel?' I say to the red-haired girl.

She shrugs, pulls her family back into the caravan.

'Let's get you into a new family,' I say, pulling the sobbing girl up to standing. Fee is there and the girl falls into her arms.

The kids are still kids, even though their world has just caved in.

As we march down the deserted main road to the bridge over to the mainland, I think back to a protest I went to in London, just after Mum went. There were swarms of kids marching down Whitehall. It seems like a lifetime ago.

The island is dead quiet as we walk out, the sky a bright blue. It feels so strange. Like it really is the end of the world.

We stop for water and snacks many times on the way, and by the time we get there, it's 4pm. The kids have been moaning for three hours, but I tell myself the end is in sight. The sooner we get off the island, the sooner we can find out what's going on, and the sooner we can get the help that we need.

The bridge to the mainland is blocked off with sand bags and rolls and rolls of barbed wire. It is manned by soldiers with what looks like rifles. Adult soldiers. The first adults we've seen in three days.

'Adults!' I say with relief. 'We're going to be ok.'

My voice cracks a little at the thought of life beyond this nowhere land.

There are four of them, about fifty metres away from us, two kneeling, their rifles pointed on us, one standing with another rifle and the other with a megaphone. They are all wearing protective clothing so we can't see an inch of their skin. Can't see their eyes. They are still adults though. They will know what to do.

We pick up the pace, and soon the kids are running towards them, all of them thinking they will explain every-thing, and take us back to our mums and dads, explain that there has been a government operation, but that it's all ok, that we're safe. The kids are desperate for things to be normal, to be rescued.

The rifles pointed towards us don't stop the children. Suddenly a voice on a megaphone blares out, which stops the kids in their tracks.

'YOU ARE ORDERED TO STAY WHERE YOU ARE. IF YOU BREACH THESE COMMANDS, WE WILL SHOOT.'

I lift my hands in surrender and shout over the barbed wire to them.

'Have you come to rescue us?' I shout. 'We woke up two days ago and our parents had disappeared. Do you know what's happening?'

The soldier with the megaphone ignores me and starts yelling into his megaphone again.

'THIS ISLAND IS SHUT DOWN. THE UK GOVERNMENT HAS DESIGNATED A STATE OF EMERGENCY. NO ONE RUNS OR WE SHOOT. DO YOU UNDERSTAND?'

'But we need help,' I say, in desperation. 'We need food.'

He doesn't answer.

Before I know what is happening, one of the boys from the caravan park, Will, the one who had asked me if there was a wild monster on the loose, runs for the barbed wire.

He gets stuck on the first roll, but then he wriggles out of his denim jacket and slips down the far side of the first roll on to the ground. He stands again and runs for the next one, launching himself over it like a spring hare, crashing down onto the tarmac.

He's running for the soldiers, wearing just his t-shirt and jeans, the adrenaline carrying him. He's desperate to be saved, like we all are.

'Will!' his sister screams. 'Will! Stop!'

'He just wants to be rescued!' someone calls out.

'He's just a kid!' shouts another child, waiting behind the rolls of barbed wire.

The soldier has his rifle pointed at the boy.

Will stops. Catches his breath. Looks as if he will surrender. Looks back at his sister. And then in a fit of craziness, pulls himself free of the barbed wire and runs for the next blockade, a pile of sandbags, behind which the soldiers wait.

He thinks they will look after him, despite what they just said, and he runs to them. A shot cracks in the air and he drops to the tarmac with a thud.

31

JAY

S unday 26th September 2021

No one moves.

Will's sister screams out his name.

We all stand there staring at his body, too terrified to move. A crimson stain bleeds through his white t-shirt.

All of us want to run to him but we're too scared.

'What the hell?' shouts out one of the boys. 'He's just a kid.'

The soldier with the megaphone turns to us.

'Why are you shooting at your own kids?' someone screams. 'We're the ones who need protection!'

'THIS ISLAND IS SHUT DOWN. THE UK GOVERN-MENT HAS DESIGNATED A STATE OF EMERGENCY. NO ONE LEAVES OR WE SHOOT. DO YOU UNDERSTAND?'

We nod, step back from the barbed wire, hold up our hands.

'We don't know what is going on,' I shout back.

'We are not at liberty to discuss anything with you.'

'But we've lost our parents, there are babies that we don't know how to care for. There are thousands of children here, with no adults. There's a dead body on the caravan site.'

The other kids start shouting too, not out of bravery but desperation.

'Where are our parents?'

'Have you taken them?'

'Have the adults gone from the mainland too?'

'You can't just leave us here, we'll all die!'

The soldier stands there motionless, deaf to our words. I wonder if getting hysterical will help the situation and then I decide against it. My sense of survival has kicked in and I'm not about to start a fight with a soldier wielding a gun.

'Ok.' I breathe deeply and try again. 'Quiet everyone!' I shout. I address the soldiers again. 'We woke up yesterday and all our parents had disappeared. Can you tell us what's going on? Is it a government thing? Have they been kidnapped? There are hundreds of children here, no help, no parents. I can't go around the whole island by myself.' I bite the tears back. 'There are children locked in houses here who will starve to death. What are we supposed to do? These kids are scared shitless, and you just shot one of them. What are you afraid of?'

'My orders are that no one leaves the island, no one comes on to the island. It is a state of emergency. You just have to stay alive.'

'But what is going on?'

'We don't know.'

'Is that it? You don't know so we're imprisoned here?'

'Those are my orders.'

'But for how long?'

'This is just the way it is now.'

'But we'll run out of food! We'll starve to death!'

I try to stir his compassion, but it seems he doesn't have any. As far as he's concerned, whatever we have to say doesn't matter.

He turns and walks away.

I turn back to the group of seventy or so kids, standing behind me. After everything, the sore feet, hunger, tiredness and tantrums, no one is coming to help us. Will's sister Leah is making a low, unearthly sound.

It seems that something a whole lot bigger than us is going on, and we don't know what. We just have to stay alive, he said.

They know the adults have gone. They know there's a whole island full of kids, just abandoned here. The military, and by extension, the government, know something crazy is going on this side of the Sheppey Crossing, and they don't want to get involved. There are other adults in the UK, though, and that answers one of my questions.

From behind our group of children, comes a noise that I haven't heard in what seems like forever, but was actually only the last two days – the revving of a vehicle. I turn to see Swanny in the driver's seat of his mum's car. He's about a hundred metres away and has that look on his face again.

'No Swanny. Stop!' I shout, and then when I realise he isn't going to stop, I yell, 'Kids! Get out of the way!'

They all dive into the hedge. Swanny's face is plastered over with a crazed look, and he's going for it, sink or swim. He revs the engine, and heads straight for the soldier.

The car is no match for the rolls of barbed wire though and it becomes wedged in the barricade. The soldiers shoot at the windscreen, shattering it into thousands of pieces. They weren't joking. Swanny scrambles out of the passenger side and runs back towards the crowd of kids, behind the shelter of the open door.

'If I see you again, I shoot!' the masked soldier shouts, firing a round into the air above our heads.

Swanny collapses next to me, trembling.

'What the hell, man?' I say.

He shakes his head.

We run back up the road, the kids all following me and Swanny. When we're a hundred metres or so away, we turn off into a field of crops. We duck in there and lie down, all sixty of us. The soldier isn't coming after us. I don't think he wants to kill us. It seems more like he is scared of us. The barricade suggests they don't have any intention of coming onto the island, it seems more a case of not letting us off. But we lie there for a while, no one sure what to do next, catching our breath, calming down. So, what? Two days ago, normal life, yesterday the zombie apocalypse, today a war zone?

I look up at the clouds where a few birds are thrown across.

The birds are the only ones who know what is really going on, I think. *The only ones who can see it all.*

Leah is hysterical. Fee holds her tight as she screams out 'Will' over and over again. Her shouts settle into muffled sobs, after a while.

Everyone is quiet then.

'Guys,' I say, 'We're going to have to walk back to the caravan park. I know you're all tired and hungry, so we'll go slow.'

'We can't leave Will here!' Leah whimpers.

'We don't have a choice.'

There are groans, but they all know we have to. We look at the food and drink that we have left between us and share it around. Crackers, apples, *Mentos, Coke, Wotsits*. Any odds and ends. It lightens the packs and gives us all a little strength.

After six, we slowly set off back up the road.

32

JAY

S unday 26th September 2021

OUR FEET ARE SORE. Our minds are blown.

Swanny, Robin, and I walk at the front of the pack, each with a child on our shoulders. I carry Kit, Rob carries Ava, and Swanny carries Max, a three-year-old. Fee is at the back chatting with the slower ones to try to keep their pace up.

'So, what do we do now?' I say, as we start the long walk back, a trail of whining children following after us, sobbing as they walk. How could I have been so foolish to think that there would be normal life on the other side of that bridge? Nothing is normal anymore.

I don't know what I was expecting. How could anything be normal after what has happened to us?

I had questions before getting to the bridge but now I just have more. What did he mean that they didn't know what was going on? Why weren't we allowed off when we were the ones who needed rescuing?

'Dunno, but they've screwed us again,' mutters Swanny.

'What do you mean?'

'Mum, buggering off like that. Leaving me here.'

'Whatever happened, I'm pretty sure she had no choice in the matter.'

'So, what, they're just gonna leave us here to die?' Rob chips in.

'Or live,' I add.

'Looks like it, doesn't it?' Swanny shrugs.

'The soldier said, "This is just the way it is now". As if things aren't going to change any time soon,' says Rob.

'Swanny, what were you thinking with the car? Got a death wish?'

'I've no idea. Didn't want to die though, I realised that much once I was sitting there in front of him.'

'You're lucky he didn't get you, that's for sure,' I say.

He shakes his head.

'I feel like I'm on drugs. Like this is all a hallucination. Do you know what I mean?'

Rob and I nod.

'We should have asked him about the internet.'

'Oh yeah.'

'I could be dead right now,' Swanny says, as if he's only just realised it.

'We know,' I add. 'Poor Will.'

'What are we going to do?' Robin says. 'Why don't they want us off the island? What's happening on the mainland?'

'Well, we saw one adult, and more besides. So maybe it has just happened here ... whatever *has* happened,' I say. 'But we'll drive ourselves mad with speculation. I know – I've done it before. We need to forget the outside world. Learn to survive on our own for a while. He gave us no indication of time, did he? Do they think we're infected with something?'

'Or that the island is? Maybe it's been contaminated?' Robin says.

'All he said was that we have to stay alive.'

'Maybe there's been a nuclear explosion. Maybe it got the adults but not the kids?' adds Swanny. 'Maybe we could swim to the mainland. It's not far at all.'

'What, swim into a firing range? No thanks,' I shoot back.

'We need to explore the west of the island,' Swanny adds. 'It's so close to the mainland that we'll probably be able to see if life is normal over there. Maybe one of us should go out tomorrow? And the prisons! Do you think we can hack into their CCTV? It'll all be on record.'

'I was there this morning. I didn't think to scroll back through it. Didn't seem to be password protected.'

Fee catches up to us. 'Hi guys.'

Swanny and Rob murmur a greeting.

'The ones at the back are flagging,' she says. 'I think we'll have to stop for some dinner.'

'We'll get back at midnight at this rate,' mumbles Swanny.

I can tell he's suspicious of her.

'They're only little,' she says, with a shrug.

Just then there is a shout from behind a wall on the housing estate we're walking past.

'Hey! Where have you come from? Mainland?'

A teenage boy emerges, holding a stick across his body like a spear. I think I recognise him vaguely from school. He's a couple of years younger than me. There are others with him – a group of about ten kids, all about his age or younger. Seems like he's the leader. They stay back from us, all in a row, eyeing us suspiciously.

'We tried to get to the bridge,' I reply. 'They're not letting anyone across.'

'Duh. We know we tried too. There's been some apocalypse, hasn't there,' he says.

'Well, there's adults on the other side of the bridge. So, we think it's just here, whatever it is.'

'We know,' he says, deflated. 'What's so special about here?'

We shrug. There's no point being macho, and he knows it too.

'So, what do we do then?' he asks.

'Stay alive?' I suggest.

He rolls his eyes.

'Do you guys have enough food?' I add.

He shrugs.

'We have a bit. How long have we got to last it out?'

'No idea. Come and find us if you want to. We're at Leysdown Holiday Park.'

The boy shrugs and his gang turn and walk away.

'They'll come later,' I say. 'Why would you want to be on your own?'

'Haven't you just exposed our entire place of safety to some total stranger?' Swanny says, angrily.

'He's at school with us. And anyway, they're just kids. We're all just kids. It won't get nasty until the food starts to run out.'

I don't have the energy to take sides against a bunch of kids who've just lost their parents. Sometimes you just have to trust in basic human goodness, don't you? Then I remembered what had just happened at the bridge and didn't feel so sure.

'What should we do?' I say, turning to Fee. She reads the kids and knows what they need.

'Let's push on a bit, another ten minutes or so?' she says.

I nod and we carry on.

'We haven't got much food,' I say to her, in a low voice. There are only a few packs of biscuits left. We ate it all back there.'

Swanny barges over to us, all blag and swagger.

'You two. Whatever you've got to discuss, you can discuss with all of us.'

I sigh. He's making it a power thing, a leader thing. He doesn't want to be left out of any decisions, but I don't trust him. He makes bad decisions. I know things have changed somewhat in the last two days, but still.

'I was just explaining to Fee that I don't know how we're going to get everyone back. We've only got biscuits. It's bloody miles.'

'Can we sleep out under the stars?' he suggests.

The thought crossed my mind too. However, the thought also occurred to me that there is something out there, on the marshes, roaming the island, something that we don't understand. What if it hadn't found what it had come for? What if it was looking for something else? I shudder. What if there is something out there, like Will had said?

'No way,' I answer and surprise myself with the fear I feel. I was used to being scared of drowning, but fear of an imagined beast, roaming this island? Making the adults disappear? That's the stuff of kids' books. I'm not scared of stuff like that. Am I? Who knows the depths of my fear?

I've never longed more for my stupid tinny caravan, for a door that locks, for the sound of the kettle boiling, for the stuffy warmth of the place, for Dad watching *Countdown*.

But then I remember, Pete's door had been locked, hadn't it? The birds had still got into him.

I'm meant to be able to cope with this. Everyone expects

me to know what we should do because I know how to deal with death and stuff. But this is different.

'Why are you listening to Fee, anyway? Where'd she even come from?' says Swanny.

I roll my eyes and mouth '*sorry*' at her, and she smiles.

THE KIDS MANAGE another mile or so before we stop for a long while. We eat all the biscuits that we have with us, and everyone has a swig of water. We're all exhausted.

I lie on my back, looking up at the clouds sailing across the sky. Kit lies next to me, his silence weighing on me. I know he's been listening to everything we've been saying, but what can we do? We can't keep it from him, we just have to figure it out as we go along.

'Is it worth trying to keep looking for people?' I say to Robin. 'I don't know what else to do now. I really thought we were going to be ok then, for a minute. I thought they were going to help us.'

'I know Jay,' says Rob. 'We all did.'

'Let's keep going with the runners – it'll keep people occupied if nothing else. They can send anyone to Leysdown Holiday Park if they need help. Break down every door, find all the kids, make families, try to stay alive. For whatever reason, they're not coming to help us, so we help ourselves.' I stand up, start pacing. 'We're on our own, sink or swim. We need to get this message to every town and village on the island.'

'Ok chill, Jay.'

'Chill?' The very word suddenly strikes me as hilarious. 'Chill?' I suddenly feel as if I'm in the Hunger Games, as if all of this is a fabricated world and we're really living out some twisted version of survival of the fittest.

'Let's not let anyone fall through the cracks this time,' I say. 'Not like Zozo, or Kit.'

'But the Island's too big to look everywhere,' says Swanny. 'Who's Zozo?'

I glare at him but don't answer. He carries on, heading off down some conspiracy theory path. 'Do you think the government took them? An underground police force, like the Stasi? How can they have disappeared? There were locked doors man, that's what I can't get my head around. What abductor can unlock doors from the outside and then locks them again after they've gone? It doesn't even make sense, it's not physically possible.'

'Nor is a secret government agency, creeping around on Sheppey, stealing hundreds of sleeping adults,' says Robin.

'What if the government had recruited them all into special service to fight this Cut Off mess?' Swanny says. 'Some golden opportunity that they couldn't say no to? Lucrative, like.'

'What, and you were only eligible if you were naked and left your clothes out in the shape of a body? Get real,' I say.

'Drastic times call for drastic measures,' Swanny says with a shrug.

By the time we get back to the caravan park, it's after midnight so the children eat whatever they can find, and Fee helps me to get them all into their families and into their beds.

Exhausted, cold and hungry, Kit and I head back to the caravan. Kit is occupied for a while with some cars that we borrowed from another family, before he gives in to tiredness and settles down in my bed to sleep.

I go into Dad's bedroom and sit on the bed again. That

thing Swanny said has sparked something in me. Had Dad known he was leaving? I look for clues – a suicide note, an explanation or trail that might lead me to an answer. Something, anything. I shift papers, look in drawers. But there's nothing.

'No,' I say to myself. 'They didn't know they were going. Dad would have told me.' I realise, that after everything that we'd been through, I know that for sure.

But where does all this leave us? All I can imagine is us dying in some awful way, starvation most likely, or exposure, or some other illness that we can't cure. How can they do this? The government, in full knowledge, leaving us here to die?

Why am I supposed to know what to do? I'm just a screw up.

I know what it is to be lost though, maybe that's what qualifies me. A calm head in a time of crisis too, because I know that panicking gets you nowhere. I've lived through a nightmare and come out the other side, some of the kids know that. But what 'other side' can there possibly be here? How can anything ever get better?

All my energy for the last two days has been spent trying to get us off the island, to get us help, but like a punch to the stomach, I realise there is no help to get.

I crash down on to Dad's bed and the tears well up in my eyes. I think of Zozo. She was the definition of life itself and death still got her.

MUM WENT to wake her one morning after sleeping in late, and she found my little sister pale and unmoving. It was August seventeenth.

'JAY!' she shouted. 'JAY! She's not breathing!'

'Shit! I don't know what to do!' I shouted, running into the room.

I just stood there staring as Mum lifted her small body out of the cot and shook her, 'ZOE! ZOE WAKE UP!' She didn't even turn to look at me as she yelled, 'Ring for an ambulance!'

They told us what to do. "Keep doing what you're doing," they said, deceptively calm. Two breaths and thirty pumps.

Dad was at work.

Mum was freaking out, she wouldn't stop.

Hyperventilating, trying to concentrate, doing the breaths and the pumps, but it wasn't working.

She sat back against the wall when the paramedics arrived. They tried to resuscitate her, but it was no good.

'She's gone,' one of them said. 'I'm so sorry.'

'What? She can't be!' Mum was shouting. 'You have to do something! You have to bring her back.'

'I'm sorry, there's really nothing we can do.'

'But you have to, she's my little girl. You have to. Please keep trying,' she begged.

But they shook their heads. And then Mum wrapped herself in a ball and howled.

I called Dad. I was the one who had to tell him, and he came running up the street, white as a sheet.

I talked to the paramedics, thanked them for trying. Then the police showed up. Hours later the coroners came and carried our Zoe out of the house.

It was fuckin' traumatic.

In a day, our life had been emptied out like an ashtray. What were we supposed to do next?

Weeks later, they called us in after the post-mortem to discuss the results. SIDS, they said.

'It's a complex thing, hard to understand,' said the doctor. 'Impossible to see it coming. Nothing you could have done.'

His words came and went like waves, sweeping past us, nudging up against us, cold and vague.

'But what am I supposed to do?' asked Mum, sobbing.

Later, as we were leaving she said, 'I swear they don't train these guys in people skills do they?'

Dad cried in that meeting. I saw the tears steal their way out of the corner of his eyes. He clenched his jaw against them coming and his fists were squeezed tight around his beanie, to stop them coming, I guess. He wouldn't let the dam break, but it was giving way. That was the only time I saw it close to breaking. He managed to stop the flood though, managed to rein it in.

We walked back down the labyrinth of corridors, numb with our sadness, then we were expelled into the muggy August heat, and that was it.

Crack on with life.

On our own again.

We cobbled together a service for Zoe which felt wrong in its entirety.

After that, there were arguments behind closed doors, early in the morning, late at night.

And then Mum stopped getting out of bed in the mornings. Dad would be up, make his sarnies and be off for his shift. He didn't talk about it but packed all his feelings down inside of him and got on with things. I used to head out of the door just after 8am to get to school on my bike. We were distracted, like, had other things to take us away from the home, the heart of the hurt. Mum, on the other hand, had an empty day ahead of her, one that she used to fill with Zoe. She couldn't bear to throw away any of Zoe's things, so she just left them in her room. All pink and fluffy like marshmallows. I came home from school one day to find her lying in Zoe's cot.

'It still smells of her!' she said, between sobs.

'Mum,' I said, awkwardly. 'Are you ok? Can I make you a cuppa?'

I'd never been good at knowing what to say. She shook her head, and I backed out of the room, not knowing how to contain her grief, or what to do with it. Of course, she wasn't ok.

She only talked about Zoe when she'd been drinking, after 11pm when the gameshows stopped.

'I don't know why she's gone, Jay. I don't know what I did wrong. You tell me, what did I do?' she said.

'Mum, you didn't do anything wrong,' I said. 'These things just happen ... the doctors said. SIDS just happens sometimes, and they don't know why.'

'But if I'd have been there with her, holding her hand, it wouldn't have happened, would it? If I'd have been there. If she had been awake.'

'Mum don't torment yourself. It wasn't anybody's fault.'

She shook her head.

'The buck stops with the mother. I should have been there for her, and I wasn't.'

'Mum, you were asleep!'

She didn't talk about it in the cold light of morning. She steeled herself for a new day; a day of silence which should have been spent cuddling, mothering, entertaining, consoling and laughing.

She was a ghost of herself. Distracted. Scatty. She tried to get herself back, she tried so hard. She took me on crazy adventures to swim in the sea after dinner, or to run as far as we could up the coast, but she was only trying to distract herself, to get away from herself.

'Did you try going to see that counsellor?' I asked her one night, when she was already well-oiled with alcohol. 'Do you want me to make an appointment for you and Dad?'

She nodded glumly, rubbed her eyes and stared at me.

'Yeah, maybe that's a good idea, Jay. I don't know how to keep going.'

There was a space the next week. The closer the date got, the more she worried about it – about what it would unearth in her. Dad shook his head at dinner when we were discussing it.

'It ain't for me. I'll deal with it in my own way.'

'But you've been given six sessions for free from child bereavement services, why not just go and see what it's like? What have you got to lose? Please just try it at least.'

They did go, just the once. I skipped school and waited outside for them. Dad came out with flushed cheeks and tear lined eyes.

'I'm not doing that again,' he said, looking at me coldly. He turned to give Mum a peck on the cheek, buttoned up his Donkey jacket, took a drag on his cigarette and walked off to work.

'See you later Dad,' I called after him.

He half-turned, half-waved and then carried on. Things to do. Somewhere better to be. He held it against me, I could tell. I had pushed him into his grief, somehow, by persuading him to go.

Work always took him away from us, from the pile-up that was mounting in our life. He was able to walk away from it all somehow. I don't know how he did it. Mum came out looking arthritic, smaller, bowed by the weight of the confession, holding the weight of her grief like a bowling ball. It weighed her down, slowed her steps.

I put my arm around her, instinctively, trying to share the weight of the burden, trying to lift her. 'Shall we go home?'

She nodded. 'Yes love, let's go home.'

'What was it like?' I asked, as we walked back to the bus stop.

She shook her head. 'It was lovely.' Her voice broke and she bit her bottom lip. 'We just talked about her. We talked about all the things she did that made us laugh.' She shrugged, biting her lip to stop the tears. 'But it made the pain bigger somehow. Illuminated it. Your dad couldn't cope.'

I put my arm around her waist, and we perched in the bus shelter, waiting for the 435 to take us home.

Mum carried on with the counselling without Dad, and I thought that she might have turned a corner, that she might have talked it out by the end of six sessions.

But six sessions wasn't very long in the grand scheme of things and she unravelled again at the end of it, like a ball of wool. She couldn't stay focused on even the littlest task; she would get distracted or give up halfway through. I came home one day to find her reeking of cider, crying on the sofa.

'I was going to cook you a nice supper,' she said, shaking her head. 'I went to *Co-op* and got all the ingredients, and when I got back I realised I forgot the chopped tomatoes. So stupid of me,' she said. 'So stupid! And then I wasn't going to have time to walk all the way back and get it, so we've got beans on toast again for supper.'

'Mum, don't worry. I can go on my bike. Shall I go out now and get it?'

She shrugged, nonchalantly. And then she shook her head.

'I don't want you to go,' she wailed, looking at me. 'I've been on my own all day!'

I looked at her, not knowing what I should do.

'I'm sorry,' she said, seeing the look on my face. 'I'm losing the plot, aren't I?'

I shook my head.

'No one should have to go through what you went through,' I said, sitting down next to her and putting my arm around her back. 'I don't know what I can do to make it better.'

'Just be you, Jay-boy, that's enough.'

She hugged me back, and I could feel her chest shaking as she cried. We walked back to the shop together and then cooked spaghetti bolognaise, not speaking much, just being together. We ate together when Dad got back from work.

'Do you remember her dancing around on the sofa to Uptown Funk?' I said. 'Zoe loved that stupid song.'

'And that time she picked up a worm and pulled it in half!' Mum smiled, and then added, 'and the way she used to corkscrew in between me and your dad in bed.'

Dad smiled and looked down at his plate of food. He finished it quickly, pushed the plate away from him and stood up.

'A few of the lads are going down to The Black Dog tonight for a few, you don't mind if I join them, do you?'

Mum shook her head and stood up to start clearing the plates. She carried them back to the sink and turned her back to us to start the washing up.

How was she meant to find a way through without booze if Dad couldn't? I wondered. How could she heal if he refused to talk about her?

I know a glass or two of wine helped her to unwind and get some sleep, but her drinking during the day made me feel sick to the stomach. The anxiety wound around my gut, and I never knew what I would get back from college to find. It was taking her down another road that was going to end badly, I just knew it. She knew it too. Choose the other path, I wanted to say to her, but I didn't. She was too fragile, and I didn't want to push her away from me.

Some days I thought I should just give them a break. I wouldn't know how else to cope if it was me who lost a child. It was hard for me, but Mum and Dad grew Zoe from their love and their loss was deeper and bigger than mine, bigger than themselves even, as deep as the ocean.

Mum didn't have many close friends. I wondered if that was part of the problem. She'd grown up at the other end of the island and moved down this way when she met Dad. Met him in a pub when she was out in Sheerness for her eighteenth. Mum didn't see her friends so much after she met Dad. It wasn't far – only 40 minutes or so but we didn't have a car and there was always other stuff to do. I cycled for college. Dad cycled to the cannery just up the coast where he drove a forklift. Didn't love it, but there weren't much choice for him, he always said.

I've heard about when they met. Mum and Dad in a bar, summer and booze. The bar closed and they wandered around town until it was getting light. Dad took her back to his parents and she met his Mum in the morning, still hung over and wearing last night's smudged black eyeliner.

Cheap wedding, by all accounts, up at the registry office in Sheppey, then a bus back for dinner at The Dog. There was a photo, her hair out of her face, a little bouquet of flowers, a blue dress.

I would lie awake at night sometimes, wishing that time

would go backwards, that they could be young and in love again. Everyone wants a mum and dad who love each other, don't they?

I could have buggered off more so they could have had more time together, but they didn't want it; instead, they anaesthetised themselves with booze and TV. I don't think they could remember how they used to talk to each other.

If only we could have turned the clock back, if only Dad could have made more effort, if only they could have talked more.

If only we'd known what she was about to do.

33

JAY

S unday 26th September 2021

FEE TAPS on the glass pane later and wakes me. I must have fallen asleep on Dad's bed. She's like fire on my doorstep; her eyes burning when she looks at me.

'Hi,' she says.

'Hi. You ok?'

She looks at me as if she wants to trust me, but isn't sure she can. Seeing her there makes me want to cry; it's all too much. I want to hold her, and to be held. I want everything to be ok again, back to normal. I want her to know that I don't know what I'm doing.

Like her name, Fee is a fairy, a half-way girl. It feels like she's not fully here, like she has a foot elsewhere. When she turns in the light, she seems opaque, breakable.

'Do you ever write?' she asks.

I shake my head.

'I walk. That's how I deal with stuff,' I say, leaning on the caravan door frame.

'I've written some poems. Can I show you?' she says.

'Sure.'

She shoves a crinkled exercise book into my hands and stands back to let me read it.

'This keel, that tips and steers the boat,

That anchors bone to bone,

Feather to heart, that gives me flight,

my superpower.' I flick to the next page.

'The feathers would scatter like petals, drop from my back, the moment I left, I know.

I would stand up and shake them, noiselessly to the ground.

And there would be new things and I would walk unfettered towards them,

Bare feet, my hand shielding my eyes, squinting into the sun.'

I hand her the notebook back. 'Yeah, they're nice, real poetic,' I say. 'It's unusual, yeah, I like it. Is it about being like a bird then?'

'Yeah, kinda.'

They remind me of Mum's poems.

'Do you want a cuppa?'

She nods.

I make her a cup of tea and we sit on the metal caravan step together. I still feel like I can't trust the outside, because whatever has done this is out there isn't it? Whatever power, whatever creature, is out there, roaming.

I can feel the warmth of her side against mine.

'I'm sorry ...' I say, turning slightly.

I can feel her eyes on me.

'I'm sorry about the bridge, about dragging all the kids out there.'

'We had to try,' she says. 'You did the right thing. You're a born leader you know.'

'No, I don't know that. But no one else seemed like they would be able to do it. I've been through stuff. I know what it's like to lose everything.'

She looks at me with something. Longing?

I lean in to kiss her.

I feel her hair, hold her face in my hands.

We melt into each other.

She pulls away and looks at me and my stomach flips. *Who is this girl?*

'I'm sorry. You're just so beautiful,' I say.

She laughs.

'Where did you come from?' I say, again.

'You've asked me that before!' she says, pulling away from me.

'Yes, but you didn't answer.'

'Northumberland. Well, my Mum's side. We're looking for Dad.'

'Where's he?'

'Stuck in the EFR. I came to the island, after I heard.'

'What? But how did you get here? How did you hear? We've been shut off, since the birds. Since yesterday.'

How could it only have been a day? Felt like a lifetime.

'There were ways.'

'What ways?' I ask, incredulously.

She shrugs.

'So where do you live?'

'Alone.'

'Why won't you answer any of my questions?' I ask, growing impatient.

She shrugs and looks away nonchalantly.

She has a strength, something that tells her she can get

through this. Perhaps she's already seen worse. Perhaps she's already a survivor. Like me, I guess.

'Ok fine, tell me when you're ready. But you still haven't told me how you got here.'

She shrugs.

'I thought I'd come this way to get to Belgium. I need to find Dad. He went for work, outside, you know?' She nods her head to one side as if outside meant outside the caravan. She means outside of the UK though. 'He went as a mediator when the Cut Off discussions were at their peak, but he never came home. Then the borders were closed and now all I know is that he's marked as missing. He worked for the British embassy in Brussels and was made redundant when the UK was sanctioned. He called us; said he would be on this flight. But he never got on the plane. Then all this stuff blew up and any chance of finding Dad has grown slimmer every day. There's an address that he gave me before he went – a safe house. He said I should go there if anything happens. So that's where I'm going. I thought it was less obvious this way, somehow.'

'What makes you think he wants to be found?'

She pauses for the slightest of moments.

'Why wouldn't he want me to find him? I have to know that he's ok. I have to go.'

She is ruffled by the thought that he may not have wanted to come home.

I knew what it was like to have a parent disappear.

'What makes you think you can get into Europe?'

She shrugs. I can't figure out where she got so much self-belief from.

'None of us are really trapped, are we? We're just choosing to stay here.'

'Are we?' I ask, incredulously. 'Please tell me how we can escape!'

'There's always a way out. We just have to find it.'

DESPITE EVERYTHING, there is hope in her eyes. She is holding on to something that none of the rest of us are, almost as if there is something she knows that we don't. I realise that's what's different about her. She's doesn't seem desperate to leave, like the rest of us are, even though she's on her way somewhere. She seems to like it here.

'I didn't tell Mum I was leaving, I just left her a note. I know I've done the same to her that your mum did to you, but if I told her where I was going, she would have stopped me, made me promise not to go.'

'Wait ... how do you know about my mum?' I ask.

'Oh,' she looks surprised. 'Um ... I was talking to Robin the other day. He filled me in.'

I frown. I've never seen Fee talking to Robin.

'Anyway ...' she rambles on, eager to switch the subject back to her dad. 'I came down to London after the Cut Off, begging at the embassies, trying to pick up Dad's trail. Then, I came out to the island when I realised the only way to find out what happened to him was to go myself. That's why I came here, to find a way to get to the EFR. And then all this crazy bird stuff happened. I saw it. I saw all the souls being lifted up. Did you?'

I look at her in horror and shake my head.

'So, you were here before the birds? You saw what happened?'

'It looked like ash going up, pale ghosts, rising. I couldn't sleep, I was so unsettled, but I knew something was going on. The birds have never come like that before. Didn't you know it was coming? Couldn't you just feel it?'

I shake my head in disbelief.

'I was dead to the world, too much lager and a black lake … So, wait, what happened?'

She shrugs.

'All I know is that the birds came, and the adults went.'

'But …' I begin, 'how are we even having this conversation? Birds don't abduct humans. They don't vaporise them. What actually happened? Where is my dad? Right now?'

'I don't know,' she says, spreading her hands in a gesture of helplessness.

'Part of me wonders if this is some kind of sick experiment,' I say. 'If this island is a model of the UK in miniature – shut off from the mainland, no trade and no support. Have the government done it to see how quickly we will implode? How quickly we will die? Are we foretelling the fate of the UK?'

She nods, as if the thought had occurred to her too.

'I just want to know where my dad is,' I add.

'I know, Jay. Me too.'

We sit there for hours, wondering about things, but as she walks back to wherever it is that she is staying, I feel a flicker of rage towards her. How dare she talk about my mum? How dare she dabble in things she knows nothing of?

There is something about her, something that doesn't stick to the rules, and much as she is beautiful, I already feel that there is something she is keeping from me.

I watch her walk away into the quietest of nights. A yawn between the days – no wind, just silence. Even the sea is quiet. It feels as if everything has shifted, as if the island is waiting for something.

Freaky the way she acted as if she knew about mum, freaky how similar their poems were.

IT WAS ON NOVEMBER SIXTH, 2018, that Mum went. I say went. Was taken. Whatever. Three years ago, now.

I've gone over and over it. It was a Tuesday. Dad had gone early for work, started his shift at 7am so I hadn't seen him that morning, but the door slamming on his way out was normally the thing that woke me.

I put my head around the door to Mum's room, and she was sitting up on the edge of the bed, in her pyjamas still but with a smile on her face.

'Morning, Mum,' I said. 'Fancy a cuppa before I go to school?'

'Yes, lovely,' she said.

I went back to the kitchen to make one for both of us and bought them back through. We sat on the edge of her bed while we drank.

'How are you feeling today?' I asked.

'I'm ok. I think I need to make some changes, time I stopped moping around.'

'Mum, you're not moping, anybody would under the circumstances—'

She shook her head and put her hand up to stop me.

'No, it's fine. I need to make some changes, get back on track.'

I loved her despite the rage, the booze, her tired body getting slowly used up and worn out. I loved her despite her rants at Dad. Because after all, she was the one who would die for me, and I knew that. She was my biggest defender in a dark world. That's the way I saw it when I was younger, and I knew that she still fought for me, despite the battles raging inside of her.

She looked at me and her eyes suddenly brimmed with tears.

'I'm so proud of you, Jay,' she said. 'Look what you've become.'

I shrugged.

'You'll always be my best boy,' she said, and pulled me into an awkward hug, my head down on her shoulder, catching the warm odour of her body, the acrid smell of cigarettes that lingered around her hair.

Thinking back, I wonder if this was her way of saying goodbye. There was no finality about it though, nothing to suggest that she wasn't just feeling a little better than normal, putting things to rights with her words.

'Alright Mum, love you too,' I said, pulling myself out of the awkward embrace. 'Shall I pick something up for tea on my way home?'

'Yeah, lovely, Jay, whatever you fancy,' she said, looking down at a text that had pinged through on her phone.

And that was it, word for word. Nothing else. No lingering look, no hidden message. I headed out of the door to college feeling positive, feeling like she had turned a corner at last.

But then she wasn't there when I got back. I called her phone, and it was in her handbag, hanging by the front door on the peg. I looked at it, and there had been a few missed calls from Dad to her that day. I looked on her internet browser history, but she'd cleared it. I read through her texts but there was nothing sent that day. I called Dad and asked if he'd seen her. He hadn't.

'She'll be right as rain, lad, probably gone out for some fresh air.'

When he came home from his shift at twenty past six that night, there was still no sign of her. He didn't like to be seen to panic, but I knew he was.

We rang the police, who told us they couldn't do anything until it'd been forty-eight hours. And so we filed it, told them everything we could think of, answered their questions: how was her mental state? Poor. Did she have money? No. Did she have friends she may have gone to stay with? No, not really. Her mum was the only person we could think of – she lived up in Minster, on the hill.

We went to visit Gran that evening – she was seventy-nine and had dementia. We didn't normally go over in the evening, in fact, we hardly saw her at all. Linda, the warden squinted her eyes at us as we pulled up and then followed us over to Nell's front door.

'A bit late for a visit, gentlemen!' she called out.

'I know, it's just ...' Dad paused, not wanting to say that Mum was 'missing'. It sounded so weighty, so serious.

'We can't find Mum,' I explained. 'She's been gone since this morning. We just want to ask Nell if she's seen her today, that's all.'

'Well, she was here the other day,' Linda said. 'She's probably just having a breather. You know, what with everything.'

Yes, we knew.

'Go on, I'll let you have a quick word with Nell,' she said. 'I shouldn't, but I can see you're worried.'

Gran was tucked up in her pyjamas in her bed with *Deal or No Deal* on the television.

'Hi Gran,' I said.

'Oh!' she said, with a look of surprise. 'Hello love!'

I wasn't completely sure if she remembered who I was.

'Hi Nell,' Dad said.

Gran smiled at him and looked over at Linda—who was lingering behind us in the doorway—for reassurance.

'It's your son-in-law and your grandson, Nell. A bit late but they've come to say night-night.'

'Oh right,' said Gran.

We pulled up two chairs next to the bed and I began.

'Gran, has Mum been to see you? Shell?'

'Shellie,' she said, and glazed over. 'She isn't happy,' she said. 'She came and went like she always does.' She moved her hands backwards and forwards across her body.

'But what did she say?'

Gran shrugged.

'Did she say where she was going?'

Gran shook her head.

'Did she kiss you goodbye?'

She nodded.

I looked at Dad and then back at Gran.

'Did you give her any money?'

She shrugged and looked at the curtains, hanging in their neat pleats over the radiator.

'Why are you asking me so many questions?' she said, with a frown of annoyance.

'Because we can't find Shellie. We don't know where she's gone.'

She nodded, reached out for me with her cool, pale hand, and said, 'You need your mum, love.'

'Yes, I know I need her! That's why we've got to find her!' I said, trying not to raise my voice. Trying not to cry.

I looked at her desperately.

'Can you remember anything else?'

'I'm sorry love, I can't. Fetch me some cocoa would you Linda?'

I nodded and swallowed down the tears. My heart sunk

like a stone inside me. If Gran knew something, there was no way we could find out. All her memories were shadowy, especially the recent ones.

We kissed her goodnight and headed for the door.

'She has money in her flat, right?' I said to Linda on the way out.

Linda nodded. 'There's some in the pot on the windowsill, but I don't know how much is there now, and I don't know how much was there before.'

'So, Mum could have taken some the other day?'

'I don't like to jump to conclusions,' said Linda. 'But it's possible.'

'Did she seem agitated?' I asked Linda on the way out. 'When you saw Mum?'

Linda paused and took a deep breath.

'She came, looked like she was in a rush, a bit like she always is, you know. Nothing out of the ordinary. Not very settled though is she, your Mum? A bit flighty, like.'

We nodded.

'And she didn't say anything else to you? Didn't do anything out of the ordinary?'

She shook her head.

'I'm sorry lads. I'm sure she'll be back. Maybe she's just gone to a friend's house. A bit of headspace?'

But I saw the doubt flicker across her face.

Dad and I drove back to the flat in silence, thinking, thinking, thinking. Trying to give ourselves reason to believe that she could do this to us. Trying to think of somewhere where she would have gone.

And that's the thing I came up against all the time. I knew she loved me. I knew how fiercely she loved me. So how could she do this?

The police combed the beaches for anything that could

have washed up, any sign of her. We stood and watched them, up at Warden Bay, with all those fossils snug in the rocks, testifying to their own existence with their bodies, pressed down and preserved, and yet apparently my Mum could disappear without a trace in 2018? It wasn't possible. I knew it in my gut.

She wouldn't have lasted long in the sea in November, they repeated to us later on that day on our doorstep.

'Yes, we understand,' Dad said. 'But you have to keep looking.'

They nodded, the Chief Inspector and his aide, who were standing on our doorstep.

'We're doing all we can,' said the Chief Inspector, holding out his hands in a gesture of helplessness.

Lower your expectations seemed to be the message. There is no hope, said their sympathetic eyes.

The police found nothing. Their sniffer dog couldn't find her scent. No clothes washed up. No sightings. No one seemed to have helped her. She left her phone and wallet at home. Inexplicably, she managed to disappear right before our eyes.

They searched for a week, that's all. A week – the price for my Mum's life. When we went to the station to complain about it, the man behind the desk mumbled something about funding.

'As if I give a fuck about funding!' I shouted, banging my fist down on their desk. 'My Mum's missing. My Mum.'

Dad put his arm around me as I broke down in sobs, and he held me up, apologised on my behalf and escorted me out of the building.

'We understand,' the police officer muttered as we left.

But we didn't understand.

I tried to imagine the heartbreak when Zoe didn't wake

up from her nap, the hole of grief that consumed Mum, but I couldn't see why she'd want to lose us too. Surely she'd want to hold on to everything that she had. Dad and me. But she didn't. She ran. Like a whirlwind, like a wildfire.

She left no trace, no note and that's one of the hardest things. Why didn't she say goodbye?

For months when I woke in the morning it took a moment or two to remember. Her loss bloomed like a bruise in me; the slow remembrance that everything was broken, that there was no way to get things back to the way they were.

Dad and I made do after she went. That's the best I can describe it. We were just treading water, waiting for her to come back. We subsisted on chips and telly. Walked along the coast, all along the edge of our hopelessness. It's what we'd do on Saturdays, and it felt like a new tradition. Out of the flat and down to the sea front and one way or the other, we'd walk and walk until our feet hurt, until the sky turned orange, then we'd come back again. It took us away from the need to talk, from the pain of all the questions. And we walked around the edges of it, giving ourselves something to do, some way to fill up our weekends without Mum in them. We weren't a family anymore, we were companions, that's how it felt. It wasn't a circle anymore, with just the two of us left behind.

It felt like we were waiting for Mum I guess, even though we knew she wasn't coming back. Waiting for Zoe, too, but we knew she was in heaven.

Deep inside, I felt that Mum had found a way to go up and get Zoe, and bring her home, and that's why she'd been gone for so long. I half expected to see them come bounding in, Zoe on Mum's back, her skinny arms tight around her neck. The thought of her growing up clawed at me. If I imagined it, it meant she was still alive. I mean, I knew she wasn't. I saw her dead in front of me. But I could feel her going on alongside us, in a different world. Heaven? Call it that if you like.

And Mum? The police officers kept saying she could have been washed out to sea, as if they were trying to put the idea in our heads. But she wasn't dead, I knew it. It just wasn't like her. She'd gone off to find herself perhaps, to fix herself, we thought. Maybe she'd come back to us, wash right back up to us, like her name, Shell, a seashell carried on the tide.

It made it easier, somehow, to imagine them together, to imagine that Mum had found Zoe somewhere, that she was with her. But that meant Mum *was* dead too, so that couldn't be true.

I still saw them together, every time I closed my eyes. Whenever I tried to sleep, I saw them, and I would lie there in the dark, trying to figure it all out, but I couldn't make sense of it.

It was only the noise of the day that distracted me from them.

Dad was different to me though, and his silence carried him. His daily routine, the lads down at work, me, I guess, in part.

Sometimes I think he never really took Mum seriously. In all her little projects, all of her dreaming, even her absolute disappearance from our life, he didn't buy. It was as if he was reserving his emotions for the real tragedy that was coming. *But this is it Dad*, I thought, *Use your energy, spend your life getting her back. You've already lost Zoe, don't let Mum be lost as well.* I didn't know how to say it to him though. He carried on, on mute. One day at a time. Concentrating on the little things. Crisis survival. Almost as if he thought she was going to walk back in any day.

We drove ourselves crazy with questions. Was there something we should have done differently? Was there some warning sign we missed? Could we have stopped her? Should I have quit college so she had more company in the day? Should Dad have taken leave from work?

So many questions.

They reeled for months. Stunting our conversations, cutting in on our daily thoughts.

On my cycle to college: *Was there something more I could have done?*

On the bus up to Sheerness to meet my mates: *Why didn't she tell us how bad it had got?*

While picking up some ciggies from Costcutter: *How could she do that to us?*

And the one that lingered, unanswered: *Why couldn't we see that she was so sad?*

But it was too late for questions, too late for all of it.

It made me think that I didn't really know her at all. But if I thought that, then it would rob all the good times as well. And I didn't want them to be taken from me.

So I had to imagine that something had taken her over, some darkness that I couldn't understand. Or I imagined that her feet just kept walking of their own accord, and took her away to a better place, with no will of her own. Or I imagine that she just went for a swim, and something went wrong.

One thing though – I know that she loved me. Because as flawed and as broken as she was, she always made sure I knew that. And that fixes and breaks my heart all at the same time.

I got some counselling too; it was free at college. It was

six months later, like, so I just had to survive before that. They only spent the money once they were sure she wasn't coming back.

I knew that talking worked. The counsellor was sweet. Neat as a button with her matching outfits. Lilac cardy and skirt one week. Navy cardy and trousers the next. She looked me in the eyes when she spoke to me, and really listened, like. Gave me her full attention. It was a revelation; I had a voice, I mattered. She helped me get it straight in my head. I was loved and wanted. Dad found it hard to talk, Mum needed to talk. She couldn't cope with Zoe dying. And now that everyone was assuming it was suicide, we talked about Mum's decision, that it wasn't my fault, that some-times there's nothing we can do to keep the ones we love with us. That depression is an illness, and we couldn't have reasoned with her.

But then I threw her, right at the end. After our six sessions, the magic number where everything is supposed to be on an even keel again, I said, 'But what if she's still alive?' and that unspooled the ball of wool right back to the start.

The counsellor didn't have the answer, I could see it in her eyes. Her job was to make my life neat, even my screwed-up life, but she couldn't.

And that's why my life hangs open, you see. It's an unfin-ished story, there is no right answer, no happy ending. How could there be after what happened?

34

FEE

S unday 26th September 2021

HE ISN'T READY.
The more I speak, the more I give away.
All the things that I know,
that he won't be able to bear the weight of yet, dear Jay.
The time is coming.
Soon he will know.

35

JAY

M onday 27th September 2021

I TALK to the kids in the morning. I try to be calm, but for all my efforts to pacify them, they had just seen a ten-year-old being shot by an armed soldier.

'Ok guys,' I say. 'We still don't know what's going on. I'm as worried as you are about your parents, about getting back to normal life. But I've got a feeling that it's going to take a long time. What happened to Will was awful – a tragedy. I think it was a warning for us. I don't know what they think happened here, or what's happening on the mainland, but we've got to stick it out for a while. This is going to become our new normal. We'll do all we can to be a family, find food, look after each other, ok? The most important thing today is to find food.'

I don't have the energy to be positive today. What is there

to be positive about? Just the fact that we're alive. Alive for what?

Swanny comes running up to me after I finish talking and starts pacing back and forth in front of me.

'I've been thinking about the food issue, and I feel like I need to be able to kill something, do you know what I mean? Like to be a man here, I need to be able to like, kill an animal. Couldn't you just murder a piece of steak?'

He's talking faster than normal, and I wonder if things are getting to him. I mean we're all feeling a little crazy around here.

'Swanny, it's fine,' I say. 'I do like steak ... but you know, you don't have to.'

'No, it'll be a crack. I'm going to get me one of the cows down the lane. Will you come and watch?'

'OK,' I say, unsure of what I am about to witness. He's trying to chip in, at least.

I ask Fee if she minds taking care of Kit for a while. She looks at me, her eyes like fire, and I feel a burning in my stomach. Even though she'd made me angry I can't wait to be alone with her again. I walk down the lane with Swanny. A few of the other kids follow us. Swanny always was a spectacle.

He stands there opposite the cow, holding a carving knife, obviously dreaming of juicy steak. And then he shrieks suddenly and runs towards it, knife aloft.

The cow just stands there. And then when Swanny plunges the knife into its neck, it bolts, taking the knife with it.

'Crap! What now?' Swanny shrieks, turning to me.

'I don't know!' I say.

He runs after the cow, and manages to get his hand on

the knife, but he can't get it out of the cow's flesh. The cow is still running and now is making an awful noise.

Swanny manages to get two hands on the knife and pull it out. He plunges it into the cow's flesh again, and then runs away, cowering, straight back to me.

'Mate. What am I doing? I mean, what have they ever done to me?'

'Swanny, don't be daft, it's only a cow.'

'I can't kill it. I don't know what I was thinking. And now I've half killed it. What do I do now? I can't stab it again.'

We approach slowly and pull the knife out. The cow doesn't seem bothered but thick droplets of blood begin to gather at the lower end of the wound.

'What, am I a murderer now?'

'It might survive,' I say, uncertainly. 'It looks pretty sturdy.'

Swanny hangs his head in shame.

'No steak, then?' I ask.

'No steak. Mate, what is wrong with me? I can't even kill a cow.'

Swanny takes the knife, blood stained and sticky, and hurls it into the hedge.

'Man, I'm sorry,' he says, and then turns to the cow. 'I'm sorry, dude! I didn't know how hard it would be to kill you!'

'All for a piece of meat,' I chuckle. 'You didn't have to, Swanny.'

'Meat can get lost,' he mumbles, and then he crumples at my feet. A hundred metres behind us, there is a row of inquisitive faces at the gate, watching us.

And there, in the middle of a field, with Swanny curled into a ball at my feet and a pissed off cow making her way back into the middle of the herd, I laugh.

Not for anything other than how ridiculous all of this is.

'Piss off, mate,' I hear him say from within the folds of his clothing.

As we walk back together to the caravan park, the other kids following, I say, 'There are other options, you know man ...' I pause. 'Like ... shit! The cannery! It'll have loads of food!'

I turn to him with my arms spread open wide.

'My dad never stopped going on about what an awful waste it was. They just locked it all up when they closed the cannery.'

Swanny laughs.

'Mackerel for life, man! Mackerel for life!'

'I hate mackerel.'

'Me too!'

'Who cares?'

We run back to the caravan park, hollering with delight.

A FEW HOURS LATER, after scaling the padlocked gates, Swanny and I find pallets and pallets of mackerel and sardines. They'll keep for years. We stuff our rucksacks full of cans but there are far more than we can carry. There is enough to feed us for months.

Later, when the kids open the cans and taste the awful taste of tinned mackerel, I laugh again, because what are the chances? A whole year's worth of food is just sitting there on pallets and it's ours for the taking.

'We're going to be ok,' I laugh. 'We're going to get through this.'

36

JAY

Octobcr 2021

I FIND a street map of Sheppey in the abandoned *Co-op* and we begin to tick the roads off, one by one. A lot of the food has already gone. We're still looking like mad for whatever we can find. It wouldn't take long to die if you didn't know how to look after yourself. We scour the land, each caravan, each lane. We send out kids in waves. We cover the island in the space of a week. We keep going with desperation and cannot rest until we know we have found everyone. There are other groups of kids that help us, little pockets of them all over the island, and the word spreads.

A lot of the kids come to join us – strength in numbers I suppose. They want to be where most of the other kids are, to pool the food and the knowledge.

A few days later, Swanny and I go back to the prisons. We scale the fence and look for a way into the CCTV system. It doesn't take long. On the front desk is a monitor, the one I saw before, which still flicks between all the cameras, and then a master pane, which has control buttons at the bottom. I don't need a log in, I just wake up the screen and pull the toggle bar back to 24.09.21.

'Woah, Swanny, it's here. We have the footage.'

We hunch closer to the screen and watch, edging the toggle bar forward from 9pm to about midnight, when we figure it must have happened.

Through the grainy footage, we can see the inmates in their beds, and then, at 11.26pm, the footage looks as if it has been tampered with. There is an almost imperceptible shadow that falls over each cell, just a little a flicker. And then the people watching TV, playing cards, lying in their beds, fall to nothingness, fall to mounds of fabric, the things they were wearing becoming all that is left of them.

'11.26pm. That's when we were on the lake, weren't it?'

'No sign of birds or anything though,' Swanny says.

'It happened so quick; you wouldn't see them anyway. I mean you can't make anything out. They were all there and then gone.'

'Could be a hoax; could be stitched together.'

'By who? And is this a hoax? You and me standing in an abandoned high security prison scrolling their CCTV.'

'No mate.'

If only there was sound, if only it was better quality, then maybe we could understand what was going on. Because what we're seeing doesn't really add up: a top security prison full of inmates vanishing, something absolutely impossible unfolding before our very eyes. Seeing it on CCTV makes it worse in a way. It feels as if the cameras are conspiring against us. To see it there on a screen make it even more terrifying, and no less unexplainable.

The receptionists, the security guards, the lifers, the parole officers, all gone. The CCTV footage doesn't give us any answers like I thought it might, it just throws up more questions.

One question is nagging at me, though. If the CCTV is linked to the mainland, which it must be, surely, then why isn't anyone doing anything about it?

We head back to the village, me with a gnawing dissatisfaction in my belly. None of this makes sense.

A ginger cat comes out of a driveway and tries to catch up to us on our bikes, but soon gives up. They'll have to go feral to survive. We'll have to start killing them if they get out of hand. I can't think about that yet, though. I think of Bernie out on the marsh and wonder if he found food today.

That night, after eating two cans of mackerel, I go back to the caravan. There's too much noise everywhere else. Kit is watching the few DVDs that we have on repeat. The Simpsons and Toy Story. I guess it blurs out reality for a while. I lie on the sofa next to him, my head spinning.

There's only one person who taught me about survival, and it was Mum. She always made a good thing out of nothing. She always had hope for the next thing, no matter how hard each day was. Her love was the thing that I grew by, the thing I measured myself by. But what was I supposed to do now, and how was I supposed to be what these kids needed when I didn't have what I needed?

She could have really been something. She had so much love. She could have helped families who had lost their little ones, she could have helped people with drink problems. But she just never seemed to be in the right place at the right time. Things didn't seem to work out for her and she ended up thinking she had nothing to give.

I do forgive her for leaving. I mean, I was broken up in

bits by it, but she was blown to smithereens by Zoe dying. All she wanted was for things to be good for us. And her one job was to keep us safe, to keep our dreams alive. And that's why she thought she'd failed. And that's why she couldn't bear to go on. Not with us, anyway. I guess she couldn't put herself back together after everything got pulled apart.

She always made me marmalade sandwiches when I was feeling poorly. She tried to get Dad into running and bought him all the gear so they could get fit together. She never quite gave up on him, even though it looked like he'd given up on himself. She used to crack up when every cake she ever made failed. She always tried to make the mundane magical, making dens with Zoe when it was awful outside, watching bad movies with me when my mates had left me out of something. She never quite gave up on us having a magical childhood, even though we knew it was a bit of a bad start where we were. She still held a glimmer of hope that we might get away somehow, that we might get off the island. I don't think she ever would have changed anything though. Dad was the agent of change because he was the breadwinner, and he wasn't fussed about leaving. She wanted to be whisked away by him, but he wasn't really the type, so she made the magic happen for us right there in the flat, right there, with the microwave meals and second-hand furniture. It wasn't everything, but it was everything we needed.

She still dreamed of escaping, and it would slip out whenever she'd had a glass or two of wine. This perfectly rehearsed version of life that she wanted for us.

One time it was pissing it down outside, and Dad had gone down the club for a Sunday afternoon beer. My mates had buggered off somewhere too, and Zozo was playing up, so Mum made us a den. It can't have been long before the day when Zozo didn't wake up.

'Like the old days, eh Jay?' she said, nudging me, with a twinkle in her eye. We got some kitchen chairs and the laundry airer out and pegged two bed sheets around it. She found some fairy lights in the box of Christmas decorations, and we strung them up and then got inside with our pillows. Zoe played around our heads with her toy food and me and Mum lay there with our legs poking out into the real world, and our heads in this fairy land that she had made for us.

'I wish it was different for you, Jay,' she said, taking my hand.

'Mum, it's fine.'

'You're a good kid,' she sighed. 'I just wish we could have done more, me and your dad.'

'Got out of here, gone somewhere quiet. I wish I could have gone to Uni.' She sighed. 'But then if I had, I wouldn't have had you, would I? And I wanted you.'

She didn't mean to make me complicit in her sadness, but it felt like that sometimes anyway. If only I hadn't been born. But she said it herself, didn't she? She wanted me.

She couldn't do her dream talk around Dad. He was bolted down to the earth and there was no changing it. He'd get so angry with her talking of changing things that she didn't even try.

'This is the way it is,' he would say, with a shrug. 'Ain't no point fighting it.'

Guarded him against any other option, I guess.

The more she spoke aloud her dreams around him, the more it pointed out his failure, whether she meant it or not, so she kept it for us, Zoe and me. She didn't want to make him mad.

I made a promise to Mum, in that tent, with Zoe playing around us.

'Promise me, Jay,' she said to me. 'Promise me that you'll get off the island, that you'll work really hard at college, that you'll make something of your life?'

'Sure, Mum,' I replied.

And after she went, that promise was the only thread of hope left here for me. I held on to it for dear life.

Funny how the things she dreamed of we almost had. I mean the sea; we had the sea! Ok so it wasn't a trendy sea, it wasn't Whitstable or Margate, but it was still the sea – prehistoric and unchanged.

Space to roam? That was another on her list, and we had space! Not our own private space, truth be told, but we had beaches, footpaths, fields.

And then there were the chickens. She always went on about owning chickens as if they were the peak of civilisation. Chickens! We never did have any. Not enough space. Dad thought she was mad.

Sure, we all wanted more – that was normal, wasn't it? But Mum carried this sadness sometimes, like she thought it was her fault, the way things had worked out.

We didn't care, we wanted her more than we wanted anything else. Screw the dreams if it meant we got to keep hold of her.

But after Zoe died things got worse, way worse. Of course, she took it on herself; it was just another thing that was her fault.

We were living in an ugly ex-council house with a back-yard that we didn't really know what to do with. It never really felt like it was ours, so we pretended that we were just making do and that there was something better coming down the line.

But the years slipped by, and when you realised that this was it, this was life, and it was slipping through your fingers, it was a slap around the face.

Dad was that islander: don't look up at the horizon, no point. But Mum just couldn't stop dreaming. So instead of coming to terms with this half-life that she had, half a family, half a heart, she walked out on us, walked out on her failure, left it all behind. That's what I've grown to believe.

Where did she go, though? Onwards into the sea? Its black open arms? Or onwards towards something else? The life she wanted – chickens, the countryside, another family?

I couldn't bring myself to imagine it, but the more I looked for her in my memories, the hazier she got, and the less I could see her at all. There's a photo I have: Dad, her, Zoe and I, down at the coast here at Leysdown. Height of summer, Zoe is balancing on the breaker, Mum holding her hands. I'm off in the background, hands in my pockets. Stupid grimace on my face. Never knew it would all be taken from me.

Still feels weird saying that now. Can't believe it's true. Just feels like that was one life and this is another. A parallel universe.

What I'd give to have Mum and Dad bickering again. What I'd give to hear Zoe doing that fake cry she used to do for attention. What I'd give to hear Dad calling: 'Come here, Shell,' when Mum got in a tizz, wrapping her in a tight hug. What I'd give to hear Mum calling 'Zozo' the way she used to.

I have fallen into a doze when there is a tap at the door. Fee. I stumble across to answer it.

'Do you want to come in?'

She nods.

I pick up Kit from where he has fallen asleep on the sofa, and I carry him through to my bedroom.

I offer her tea or coffee but as soon as I am walking back towards her, our eyes meet, and then our lips. Our hands undress each other and soon we are on the sofa, tangled in the sleeping bag, our skin touching, our bodies meeting.

I wonder if she can tell it's my first time.

I smell her hair, feel her ribs as she rolls over on to me. We melt into one and for a moment there is nothing else in this world that I want. Only her. Only now. Only this.

37

JAY

O ctober 2021

I CAN'T GET her out of my head after that. I can't stop thinking about the scent of her hair and her piercing eyes.

She left that night without speaking and I haven't seen her for two days.

Then at dinner, she is there on the other side of the field, helping the girls to make stew.

'Fee!' I say, running over to her. 'How are you? Where have you been?'

She shrugs, turns from me.

'Can we talk?' I say.

'Not now.'

'Have I done something to upset you?' I say, surprised at her coldness.

She shakes her head.

I leave her be and then after dinner, I find her tending to the fire, alone.

'Fee, are you ok?'

'It won't work.'

'What do you mean? It was perfect. You are perfect.'

'No. The kids need us. We're not here to fall in love.'

'What are we here for?'

'You don't know anything about me,' she says, turning away.

'But I want to know you. I want to be with you.'

She shakes her head.

'It's not right.'

And I let her walk away from me feeling like a hole has been punched in my chest. Nothing had ever felt more right in my entire life.

JAY

October 2021

WE BURN the caravans that we can't use. Pete's with his body still inside, and Kit's aunty's van, which is too filthy to be used for anything. We can't use them for housing, and we don't know what else to do with Pete's body. I wasn't going to dig a grave.

Swanny siphons off some petrol from an abandoned car, and we chuck it through the doorways and watch the caravans burn themselves to the ground.

We stand there watching them, and I feel numb. A little dead inside. It's like some twisted version of bonfire night. They can see us burning, I think. The EFR ships, the whole of Kent. They can see the fires, and still they don't come to help us.

But as I watch the fires burn, I also know it means the old life has gone and the new one is just beginning.

With all the empty houses, we could live like kings. They are a sign of the time before though. The caravan park suits us better. We're closer, we can look after each other better this way. It feels impermanent too, which I like; a sign that we'll be leaving one day.

Some of the kids do slink off in groups to the houses though. Swanny couldn't live in a group he told me, and despite what we were all having to put up with, I let him. I understood there was only so much he could handle. He was valuable to us in a different way. He's started looting the empty houses, systematically.

Fee is distant. She doesn't talk freely to me. I love her more than anything and I'd give anything to have her feel the same. I suppose she's right in a way though, our first job is to keep the kids safe.

Sometimes it feels like no small miracle that we're all still alive. It's the dusk times that get me; the times when all around there's the soft light and children playing. They've remembered how to play, despite everything. There are fights, but no one is excluded. No one is to be told they're not wanted, not since that fight with the girls. We've got into the habit of gathering in the field to say good night to each other before we go off to our own caravans. It's sweet, but I know there's a darkness at its heart – that the kids are afraid they'll wake up to more people gone.

Sometimes I feel as if I might go crazy, sometimes it feels like a new world, one where we're undoing everything that we learned the wrong way. I dare to believe that we're being reborn again, learning a new way of living. We've never been allowed to just *be* before. Our adults always hampered us. What would have happened if they'd just let us be who we wanted to be? And what happens now? Can we make it? Can we survive on our own?

. . .

THERE HAVE BEEN LOOTING missions to the shops – all the shops we can reach by bike anyway. Then Swanny and his lot start on the houses. At first they try to match keys to cars but it doesn't take long before he gives up. There's no fuel anyway so we leave them to the grass and the rust. We don't need them anymore.

After we loot the shops for all they're worth, and after the rats come in to clear up after us, we know we have to start planning for the future. We need to start planting seeds though the prospect of feeding a hundred or so kids from a packet of seeds seems unlikely.

We know there's plenty of food all over the island, we just have to find it. We knew there'd be cupboards in all the houses; jars and packets that wouldn't go off for years. Sooner or later, it would run out, though, and what then?

Swanny, Rob and I go down to the prisons again, knowing that there must be food there. We walk around the perimeter, until we find what looks like the kitchen area. There's a row of catering bins lined up by the back door, stinking of rotting food. There is a rectangle air vent just above the door. I lob a rock at it, and it falls out of place. I swing myself up and get a hold on it.

We crawl along it until we can see the kitchen beneath us. I can easily dislodge the grate and then climb down to the kitchen. Thank heavens they cooked tinned crap in there. There are tins and tins racked up in the pantry and bags of flour. The tins will keep for years. We push open the fire exit and drag out as much as we can, load it up into a wheelbarrow. We nick some of the prison cooking pots too, they have these huge vats which are just what we need. Back at the holiday park, we've rigged up a kind of barbecue – a brick-built stand with a ledge for wood and a grill. We manage to balance the vats on top and cart it back to the caravan park.

IN THE FIRST FEW WEEKS, the thing I missed the most (apart from Dad) was a piece of crunchy but soft toast, dripping with butter and honey. There'd been nothing to bake with, but now we have flour, the kids take it in turns to make flatbreads. We put a metal sheet above the fire and toast them over the heat. We make great piles of them; they aren't quite like bread but there's something so moreish about the chewy dough, hot from the fire, and warm in your belly as the cooler days start to set in.

THERE ARE daily expeditions to find what we need – gas, food, medicines, but things are thinning out and we're having to go further afield. We know there is a finite supply of everything. If anyone does anything stupid, we just have to hope they'll get better.

Sophie and Josh come to my door one night, carrying Tilly. She's bright red and writhing in pain. They want me to show them what to do, but I don't know. I try to hold her, to rub her stomach, but she's getting more and more distressed. Her body is covered in a red rash.

I take her out into the cool night air, and jig her up and down, holding her tightly. The night air cools her slightly. I remember Mum doing this with Zoe.

Sophie and Josh look exhausted. I tell them to go and get some sleep and I stay up that night, holding her, making her some formula, calming her if I can. All through the night, I'm thinking, *This baby's going to die and then I don't know*

*what we'll do because all the kids will know I'm just making it up,
that I don't know what I'm doing* but it's just a fever and she's
over the worst of it in a few days. The rash fades and she
settles again.

There are so many bridges to cross though, so many
what ifs. And if my mind goes down all the pathways, it'll
exhaust itself. What do we do when the formula runs out?
What if we run out of food? What if someone gets sick and
needs antibiotics? What if someone gets cancer? What if the
wild dogs go mad with hunger and attack us? I can't sleep at
night. There are so many things to worry about. Some
nights, I think I'm going crazy. All this responsibility, all
these kids.

This whole island, all to ourselves.

SOMETIMES I WONDER who is giving us this freedom, and
why? And then I realise I'm shit scared with no power to
speak of at all. Although, it does remind me of that other
time us kids thought we had power, the protest.

After Mum went, I felt like I was on sinking sands. Robin
said he was going up to London for the Extinction Rebellion
protest, said I should come, take my mind off things. I didn't
even know what we were protesting about, but I went along
for the fun.

There was something gathering as we pulled into
Victoria station about 11 am, some magnitude that was
drawing people, some power to the people, the masses.
'Rebellion Day' they called it. It felt like something was
being let loose.

As soon as we got off the train, I could feel the drawing
of crowds, of energy. I could feel the rage rising and here
was a way to let it out. It was restricted in these grey streets

and tall buildings, funnelled like a rushing river, and the restrictions gave our voice more power, more fury.

It wasn't climate change I cared about, it was being young, being robbed. It was having no chance, growing up on that island, where there was no way out. It was all the tide of stuff that had washed up at our door, that we had no way of dealing with. It was all the things that had happened to me. It was Dad's lack of vision, his small-town life. It was Zoe. It was Mum.

We marched with purpose down Victoria Road, past the faceless city buildings, peppered with *Starbucks* and *Pret-a-Mangers*. We walked on the road and didn't care – there was enough of us to turn into a mob, an army if we wanted it. The masses turned down Horseferry Road towards Lambeth bridge where we gathered and made ourselves as tight as a Roman legion, spreading out across the bridge, stopping the traffic. We were aiming for a peaceful protest, but the rage was growing. The more we chanted, the more it rose up in our guts, the anger and the injustice.

Could I let my rage out here, I wondered; was it allowed? I could have screamed my guts out for days. I could have lay there on the pavement and sobbed.

We linked our arms and chanted all morning and for once I felt part of something to be proud of.

Police officers stood by, redirecting the traffic. They didn't think we were a serious threat. They didn't care what we had to say; we were just kids, weren't we?

They said they would arrest us, but we scarpered then, and joined the other kids from around the capital. We turned right onto Millbank and then followed the road up to Trafalgar Square. More kids were joining us all the time, we got stronger and stronger as we walked.

I let out a holler that sung out from the very depths of my lungs. This is what it meant to be alive!

I had joined them.

This mess, this glorious capital city mess was what I wanted. It made my heart buzz to be alive, to be a part of this swarm of humanity, full of anger, bodies pressed in against bodies, rage pressed against rage.

I was carried along by the wave of bodies and was so busy chanting that it was a while before I realised I couldn't see Rob anywhere. I stopped dead in the flow and tried to make my way back up the street the wrong way to find him, my eyes flicking this way and that over the crowd, the angry faces. I was trying to push against the flow, moving upstream, when everyone else was moving downstream. Each step felt like wading through a deep river, the bodies pushing past me were the buffets from the currents.

I locked eyes with a woman wearing a pink hoodie, pulled down low over her forehead. The tide of bodies jostled her away before I realised who it was. Mum.

Was it? It could have been. She looked, for a moment, as if she knew me. Then she was gone.

I made my way to the edge of the flow of bodies, elbowing my way through. I got to a lamp post on Whitehall and held on. I turned, to watch the swarming mass move away from me, an unstoppable tide down a one-way street, heading to Trafalgar Square. I felt dizzy.

'Mum,' I called weakly. 'Was that you?'

I waited a few minutes and caught my breath, and then climbed some steps to see if I could make out Robin but there was no hope. There were thousands of protesters. I texted Robin, told him I'd see him back at the station. No way we'd find each other in this.

The kids sat in Trafalgar Square, chanting and shouting

all afternoon. Megaphones and crossed legs everywhere you looked.

'This is what democracy looks like!'

'The sea is rising and so are we!'

I legged it when the cops threatened to arrest us all in Trafalgar Square – didn't fancy it with everything else going on. At least they gave us fair warning. It made their job harder to arrest us anyway. I ran all the way back to Victoria, and found Robin again, waiting for the 7pm train back to the island. We climbed on board in a daze of excitement and exhaustion. I felt spent and it was a good feeling. We stank of BO and our voices were gone but we had hollered for all that we were worth, all day long. It felt good to be spent.

The train carried us out of the swarming city, and as we pulled away, I noticed a homeless man near the tracks. He looked stoned out of his head. He was wearing a dirty old coat and dancing around with holes in his shoes. It was freezing cold in November, and there he was, looking happy as anything. What right did he have to smile, I wondered? What right did anyone have? He must have had so much taken from him, and what did he have to speak of now? He had found a little happiness, though, from somewhere, and it made me wonder if I could find a little for myself too.

The day faded, and soon enough, all I could see were the streetlights blurring through the window, but brighter and more garish than that was the reflection of myself against the dark pane.

I was too tired to talk to Robin and both our voices had gone anyway, so we looked out of the windows and scrolled on our phones until we got back to the island.

I wondered if it really was Mum that I had seen, but the entire day was so out of the ordinary, that you could have told me anything and I would have believed it. I didn't tell

Robin. I might have imagined it, and also, I didn't want to cry. Some things were best left unsaid.

We arrived late, and Robin's Mum lost her shit when we told her we were going to miss the last bus, and also that my dad had already had too much to drink so could she come and get us? She had to get Ava out of bed to come and pick us up. Ava seemed to think it was a great adventure. She also thought watching Robin get blasted by their mum was hilarious, so she didn't mind at all. And I could tell that Rob's mum didn't really mind either when she saw us. She just wanted him safe. Me too, I guess.

That night, I didn't tell Dad that I thought I saw Mum. I didn't want to get his hopes up. But I couldn't help wondering: if it was her, did she see me? Did she run from me again? It lit the flicker of a flame though; that I might find her one day, that the hope was not completely gone.

That outside the island, anything could happen.

39

———

JAY

Wednesday 8th December 2021

WHEN RONNIE, my second-in-command realizes the internet isn't going to be reconnected anytime soon, he gets it into his head that he can escape. He keeps going on and on about it with his mate, Weaver, who's a couple of years younger than him. Ronnie is obsessed with the idea that there is something on the island. Like Will was. Some animal or something. I don't want to be all 'I am your leader' but it's getting out of hand. I think he's cracking up.

'We know it's not that far to shore,' I say, in the morning meeting, 'but we have been specifically warned not to leave the island. It's not as if we respect the government but for whatever reason, they're pretty adamant about it. So guys, don't try to leave. You all saw what happened to Will.'

But Ronnie won't let it go. I can see the idea tormenting

him, playing on his mind. I watch him from afar and can see he is distracted as he goes through his chores.

'Mate,' I say to him later. 'You won't do anything stupid, will you? It won't end well. I can feel it in my gut. You won't get there. I know they're watching us.'

'No, mate.' He laughs. 'I'm not that dumb.'

'Ok good,' I say. 'I know this is hard, it's the hardest thing we've ever been through. It will come to an end sometime. It has to.'

'It will? When? Are we going back to the bridge? What *is* the plan, Jay? Because it seems like you're the leader that everybody wants but you're not actually doing anything, are you?'

I turn to look at him and am taken aback by the anger in his eyes. He looks at me with cold hatred, as if I'm the one who has done all of this.

'We're surviving, Ronnie, that's what we're doing. For as long as it takes.'

'Yes, but when is anything actually going to change?'

I don't have an answer. He storms off into his caravan. He is one of the few who refused to have any kids live with him. He said he'd take night watch duties instead, so he stays up all night, sleeps all day, games in the few hours that he's awake for. We hardly see him.

A FEW DAYS LATER, Fee suggests we all go down to the shore for a bit of fresh air. The weather has been getting everyone down. The winter is brutal already – it's taken the heart out of the place. We hardly ever come down here now, there's always something that needs doing up at the caravan park.

Some of the kids run on ahead of us and as we turn onto the sand, the kids run and come back screaming.

'Oh shit,' says Fee, scanning the beach, and there's nothing she can do to stop the other kids from turning to see. There's a body. Face down on the sand. Burgundy gilet, khaki trousers. Ronnie.

He must have made a break for it last night.

'Damn it,' I shout. 'I told him not to go.'

It's as if he's been planted there, where they know we will find him. He has bullet holes to the chest. Another warning.

It's almost as if they've been listening to our conversations. Can it be a coincidence?

Fee gathers the children and goes back to the caravan park. Robin and I find a tarpaulin and wrap him in it. It takes us all day to dig a hole deep enough.

'Fuck's sake,' I say halfway through. 'I warned him not to do it.'

'I know,' Robin says. 'But it was his choice.'

After Ronnie, no one talks about leaving anymore.

No one talks about boats at all. We sometimes see boats on the horizon, fewer as the months pass. We don't know if they're friend or foe. We don't know whether to wave for help, or to pretend we haven't seen them.

OVER THE NEXT FEW MONTHS, the grass starts to come up on the roads, and in the cracks in the tarmac. It grows up through the abandoned cars, still in the place they were last used, their tyres flat. Rust begins to bloom like flowers along their bodies and although it's not really been that long, the way things used to be seems so far away, and so far behind us that we can't remember it anymore.

I used to be so scathing about the gulls, and how they had this place to themselves in winter, how they acted as if the sky belonged to them, but now, it really does. The sky and the land. They've got it all. I walk past Aunty Suzie's shop and wonder what happened to her. I looted her flat but there was no sign of her, no clothes laid out like the others. I take a jar of liquorice. Most other stuff has already gone.

We don't need the rows of houses, the dockyard, the factories, the prisons, the power station. We don't need any of it, we just hide in our little patch and become industrious.

The fields up the coast were already planted up with potatoes so we dig them up, a few at a time. Boil them up and make gallons of mash, to go with our tinned fish. There are fields of cabbages too. We figure we'd better keep eating greens seeing as there's no doctor. We pilfer seeds from the farms too. Swanny found some in an outbuilding – and on a much smaller scale, we grow some spinach and sow some carrots in our makeshift patch on the caravan park.

Some days I wake, and it feels like the ground is throbbing with something new. Freedom? Rest? Being let loose, or given a break? The birds have it back, maybe that's the way they wanted it all along. It's just us kids now, living off the land the best we know how.

The longer we stay, the more we really see each other.

The longer we wait for someone to come and rescue us, the more we understand how to live.

We grow up a little, spread out a little. We communicate every day – 9am at Leysdown playground, it has never changed. We update everyone on any news. Or we just say well done, we're all still ok, does anyone need anything? The runners spread the information to those who don't make the meetings.

Some days, I wonder how it all got to be so different. I had wished for another life for so long, but this wasn't what I'd hoped for.

Some days, I wake and realise how quiet it is, like that very first morning when everything changed. There is no background noise to our days. No hum of cars, no peep-peep of the train. It's just us and whatever noise we make. We realise how much noise the adults had made with their radios blaring out, their cars driving. And we realise that perhaps we like it more like this.

JUST KIDS, whiling away our days, trying to stay alive.

WINTER DEEPENS and it's harder than anything. We still live outside; we just wear more clothes. We rig up big tarps so we can still be together, even when it's pissing down with rain. There's always something to do, some mission; planting seeds, cooking, looking for wood. The simplest stuff of life seems to spread out and fill up all of our days. The kids get used to it, toughen up over time.

We're living on borrowed time, though, and we all know it. We reached the end of the flour a while back and now it's just potatoes and fish and whatever cans we have leftover from the prisons. The runners are going further and further to find food. We're nowhere near self-sufficient. What will we do when the food runs out? The more I think about it, the more it feels like there's a mad butterfly trapped in my chest.

40

JAY

Sunday 6th February 2022

AND THEN ONE DAY, the power goes out. There is a bang, and all the streetlights go out, all the security lights, the caravans, the fridges.

Blackout.

We don't know what it means. Have they been watching us all this time? Is there still CCTV on the island? Are the boats still hovering, keeping tabs on us? We'd stopped looking for them months ago.

The kids don't mind so much about the TVs – they were only for watching DVDs anyway. There are always things to do in the evenings. Cooking takes hours. And then we have to wash up. We have a fire, and the kids play about, and then, when it's dark, they go to their caravans, and rest for the night.

But the moment the power goes out, I feel eerily

connected to that other world, the one we stepped out of on September 24th, 2021. It means they're still aware of us, that perhaps they still think of us.

So why have they turned it off? Have they written us all off as good as dead? Are they fed up with state sponsoring our existence? Have they given up on us for good? Or was it their measly support plan for us? And now they are taking that from us as well? They know we're still alive.

41

JAY

S aturday 19th February 2022

I'M MAKING some hideous version of mackerel stew again on the fire, and I look around for Fee, but there's no sign of her. I think about her all the time. I long for her. She spends the night with me sometimes, but she doesn't need me like I need her. I seem to spend most of my waking hours thinking about her, but she always feels at arm's length, looking else-where, focused on something else. I ask some of the girls if they've seen her today, but they shake their heads. I leave Rob in charge of the stew and follow the track that leads to Warden. She goes that way sometimes. I soon get to the coast, and she's there, coming back towards me, red-faced, a blue rucksack on her back, legs astride a borrowed bike.

'Fee! You ok? Where have you been?'

'Oh, just felt like a ride, that's all. I'll go and get started on the bread with the girls,' she says, and moves past me and on towards the caravan park.

I turn to watch her go, not quite able to put my finger on what just happened. She seems different, more closed than normal. As if she's keeping something from me.

Later that night, Swanny comes over. We don't see him that often anymore – he has new obsession: slow looting. He's taking his time, raking through the houses for things that could still be worth something to us now. He won't take responsibility for the kids, but every now and then, he turns up with something surprisingly useful. Antibiotics, a radio, a new gas bottle.

Today it's cans of lager, which suits Rob and me to the ground. We sit in the middle of the field, the kids playing around us, and light a fire. There's no getting away from the kids, now, this is just it, the way it is. We breathe slowly as the beer slips down our throats, and as the light falls, it's easy to imagine we're on that rowing boat again, before any of this.

'Seems a while since we last did this, lads,' Rob muses.

'Huh,' I say. 'Yeah, a lifetime ago.'

'This girl of yours,' Swanny says. 'Seen her, didn't I? With some bloke up at Sheerness few days ago. You sure she's into you?'

I don't know what to say but feel a stab of betrayal in my chest.

'What? Oh right,' my words fade as I try to hide my heartbreak. 'We're not *together,* just mates.'

'Yeah, right! Course you are. I've seen the way you look at her. She might be playing you, though, is all I'm saying.'

Every day since that first night we were together I've been longing for her to wake up, look at me, want me. Every night I long for her to come to the caravan to be with me. I've never quite given up hope.

My thoughts carry themselves away: *Of course she's too good for me. Of course she doesn't really want me. Of course she has secrets from me, what do I expect?'*

The lager soothes me into a stupor.

But it makes me realise too, what do I have if not her?

LATER, when we've sunk the lagers, Swanny and Rob have headed home, and the kids have got bored and gone into their caravans, I decide I have to talk to her. But how?

I walk down the track again, leaving Kit asleep in our caravan. I look for signs of the living amongst the abandoned buildings.

She has always kept a little distance, but for the last few weeks she's lived apart, answering to herself alone. I wonder why. She gives herself to the community all day, but when the kids are in bed, late at night, she retreats to her own place, to be alone.

I think about her and this other bloke and the rage bubbles up inside of me. *How could she do this to me*, I wonder? *Is she betraying the community? Giving away our secrets?*

Perhaps I've never really known her, I think. She reminds me of a wild animal on survival mode. Fight or flight. Eyes wide open, sleeping lightly, always jumpy. The way to survive.

I start to call out, denying the lingering fear of the dark, of being outside, on my own.

'Fee! Where are you?'

It is dark and the sea whispers. I shiver.

There is a fluttering to my side. A starling lands on the

fence post next to me. It looks at me with a cocked head, its beady eyes shining in the darkness. It is as if it has come in answer to my call.

'What do you want?' I whisper. 'Why won't you birds leave us alone?'

It looks at me for a while, and then it flies away. And I am alone. A shiver passes up my spine, because I feel like it knew the answers if I had been able to understand.

I stand still and listen for a moment, right where I am, on the dark footpath up to Warden. Brambles trail over the path, and the sea is a steadying *shh* in the background. It reminds me of Mum and the way she used to shush Zozo back to sleep in those early days, rocking and rocking her, for hours on end.

The sea rocks us islanders all to sleep as it traps us. It pacifies us, so we forget the rage. It makes us feel small, so we forget to fight. Then again, perhaps it's doing us a favour. I sometimes wonder what is happening in the world, whether things are still going from bad to worse on the mainland.

I had needed to stop being so desperate to get off the island for so long. To stop being so angry at Dad. I needed to stop going around in circles of despair about Mum and Zozo. I just needed to stop. Well, I stopped. Those crazy birds, or whatever the hell had happened, made sure of that.

Before the birds, our whole country was boiling with rage and out of options for action. We were boiling ourselves to a frenzy with no way to let off steam.

But now, here at least, the pressure has all gone. No one cares if I go to uni. I have no one to prove wrong. Not even Dad. I have no one to be angry at, even. It's just me, Jay. Just here, in this dark night, listening. Funny that. Nothing to prove anymore. Nothing to want either.

There is a rustling on the path behind me.

I turn, my heart beating faster, and see a face emerge from the shadows.

'Jay!' Fee says, brightly. 'What are you doing out here?'

'I came to find you. I was worried.'

'I'm fine. I don't mind being on my own.'

'But I miss you. Don't you want to stay with us on the caravan park?'

She shakes her head.

'I want you to be there,' I say. 'I miss you.' But she is her own and no one else's and I know it. I can't stop thinking about what Swanny said though and I have to find out the truth. 'What have you been up to today?'

'Oh, you know, played with the girls, went for a walk. Nothing major.'

'You've been in Sheerness with some bloke. Swanny saw you.'

She looks at me. A look of surprise and then sadness. I've found her out, and now I've backed her into a corner.

'Look Jay, it's not what you think, ok?' she says, as if that's explanation enough. 'I need to get back.'

I grab her wrist as she passes me, and she breathes in sharply and then looks at me, as if she is scared of me.

I let go, shocked at myself, shocked at seeing that look on her face.

'I'm sorry, Fee, I ...'

She looks at me, and then turns and runs.

42

———

FEE

S aturday 19th February 2022

I RUN FROM HIM, but he doesn't scare me,
there's just so much that I haven't worked out how to tell him.
If he backs me into a corner, it will all come out, I know it will,
and I don't know if he's ready for it.
I still love him, but I cannot let myself be a lover, not now.
I need to stay alert.

LITTLE DOES he know that although they helped me,
they cannot help me in this,
these feathered friends that he curses for everything.
I have a fatal flaw.
Little does he know that I am the weakest link on the island.

*Little does he know that when the power went out, so did my
lifeline.*

Little does he know how I got here or why,
but that I am as helpless as any of those disappeared adults.
These birds, they are the masters,
they do what they like.
I cannot bend them to my will,
I am their servant; I go where they please.
I turn into feather when they will it,
and then I become one with their multitudinous mind.
On my own, I am nothing, I am weaker than weak,
just a girl with a body that doesn't work on its own.

43

JAY

T hursday 24th February 2022

A FEW DAYS LATER, I wander out to Nan's beach house down at Shellness. The sky is a blue bruise, ominous and wounded. I come out here sometimes when I need to get away from everyone. I've not been for weeks, but I need it again, the feeling of quiet, the absolute peace. You can forget about it all being out here. I walk the few miles, cross the shingle, climb the breakers and she is there, sitting on the shore.

'Fee,' I call, so happy to see her that I forget I was angry with her.

'This is my Nan's house – did you know?' I say, pointing up to the beach house behind me.

She shakes her head.

'No, I didn't know but that sounds about right. It feels like you.'

I sit down beside her on the shore. 'Why are you so mysterious?' I ask, nudging her with my elbow.

She shrugs.

'I guess I need to protect myself. Don't grab me like that again, Jay.'

'I'm sorry, I don't know what I was doing. I just ... I miss you. I want to understand you better. I want us to be together, like that first time.'

'Jay, you don't know the half of it.'

'But I want to know all of it. Why don't you feel safe with me?'

She shrugs again, her eyes brimming with tears.

'I just want to be with you, Fee' I say.

'Then you have to let me be who I am.'

I nod, my hands absentmindedly building towers of pebbles.

'I guess I find it hard to believe that you actually want me. You've been holding back for so long. So, when Swanny says he saw you ...'

'Swanny!'

'He said he saw you with another guy, so of course I thought: why would you want to be with me?'

She shakes her head.

'Jay. You don't own me. But it's not what you think.'

'Well, try me,' I say, waiting.

She sighs.

'I can't. You wouldn't understand.'

'Well, know this. I trust you. Tell me when you're ready. If you want to.'

She nods.

'There's just one thing. You said you came after the birds, but you can't have, it was impossible. Everything was shut down.'

She sighs. 'You wouldn't believe that either.'

'How would you know if you don't tell me?'

'Ok. One thing at a time.' She tucks her hair behind her ear and looks straight at me. 'I'm one of them. We are changelings. There are some of us that can go between.'

'Wait,' I say. 'Some of who that can go between what?'

'Birds. We can go up and down. But I can't control it. That's how I got here. The birds brought me here.' She pauses. 'I know it sounds ridiculous.'

I stare at her.

'That's also how I met your Mum.'

'What?' I say angrily. 'Don't mess with me.'

She holds her hands up.

'I am not messing with you, I swear. The birds have taken me up and I've seen her, your dad, and Zoe. I told them that you're ok. They're happy, Jay.'

The tears come, then, to my eyes.

'They're ok? They're together? The birds have taken them?'

'They ARE birds, Jay.'

My parents are birds? Zoe too?

Who is this girl that has come and turned things upside down, who knows things about my mother that I don't even know? Who sees the loneliness in me, and sees the thing I long for, most of all?

THAT NIGHT, I sleep like a baby. Part of me doesn't even care if it's a lie. She has the answers, after all these years. To everything. Mum. Dad. Zoe.

And Fee ... is she a bird too, a changeling, like she says? It can't be true, but then how did she get to the island? And all the adults disappearing is impossible but that still happened so who knows what's true anymore?

It has always seemed like she is never fully here, and now that makes sense; she has one foot in bird land.

'So, you can talk to the birds?' I ask her when we meet next.

She shakes her head.

'It's not like that. I can't call them. I can't make them do anything. I think ... they just saw my need. They helped me get here because they knew I needed to get to my father. Perhaps this is the only way I'll make it. Perhaps it will end the Cut Off. If only I can get to him again.'

'What makes you think you could find your dad, even if you could get across the sea?' I ask her.

She shrugs. 'I'd sooner die trying than never know.'

I believe her.

'So how are you going to get to Brussels to find him? Can you fly?'

'I already told you – it's not that simple. No, I was going to take the boat out at the beach house. Did I tell you I'm half-French? My dad is French, that's how he can do his work out there, undercover. I have a French passport and my French is fluent, so I'm sure I could get to him. I just need to see his face again.'

I know that fierce longing because I've lived with it for years.

'I'll come with you,' I say, and I know that I mean it before I've even really thought it through. I would do anything for her.

Her eyes light up as she turns to face me.

'Are you sure, Jay? After Ronnie? You'll be risking everything.'

I nod.

I'm all in.

44

FEE

T hursday 24th February 2022

HE SAYS YES. I can rest my bird heart. He believes me. Either that or he sees no other way that I know about his family.

But now my body gives out. I can feel the strength leaving me, the thirst driving me crazy.

Will we make it across the sea?

What if I don't even get that far?

We must go soon; I haven't told him yet.

It must be soon.

45

JAY

F riday 25th February 2022

FEE and I go down to the shore the next night, while Kit is playing games with another family.

'What is it about you,' I say, holding her face with my hands, 'that is so otherworldly? You've always seemed so ...' I pause. 'Close to the edge somehow.'

Tears line Fee's eyes. She looks so tired.

'I'm dying,' she whispers.

I frown, and my jaw drops open despite myself.

What?'

'That thing I didn't tell you the other week – I'm diabetic, and I need insulin. I ran out weeks ago. I've been stealing from the pharmacies, and I can't find any more.'

I look at her aghast.

'That's where you've been disappearing off to?'

She nods.

'Why didn't you say anything? I would have helped you.'

I notice then her lips are cracked and dry, her face flushed.

'I didn't want to burden you. I didn't want to be weak. There's nothing you could have done anyway. I haven't been eating much, it'll give me a few more days. But I need insulin soon, it's beating me.'

The day the power went out was the start of the end for me. I think they cut the power because they think we're all dead. Since that day, I've been on borrowed time. I need the insulin to be cool. Without a fridge, it goes off within a month. I was buying some from that guy up in the north of the island, but he's dry now too, so ... I'm out of options.'

'What can we do? Let's take the boat, try to get to Kent?'

She shakes her head.

'If we go to Kent, we'll never get out again. I need to go to Belgium.' She paused. 'It's far though – thirty hours or so by boat. You've sailed before, haven't you?'

I shake my head, and think of the water, black and unyielding, and it makes me feel sick.

Here we are again, again, again.

'I used to swim.' I pause. 'But that was before Mum. People think she drowned. I haven't swum since. It's been years.' I falter and start again. 'I know I *can* swim because I got my lifesavers badge, I just stopped because of Mum. I'll do it for you, though. There's no other choice. I'm not the best swimmer,' I say, working out my thoughts externally, 'but I used to be. And I'm sure I can be again.'

I stand up and run into the water, fully clothed. Fear has stopped me for so long, but I have to do this, for Fee. And because I have to, I'll find out if I can.

The cold, grey water holds me in its grip. It takes my breath away and I can feel myself sinking but then I picture

Fee holding me up. I imagine Mum, Dad, and Zoe, as birds in the sky above me, swooping and darting above me, holding me aloft. I duck under, let the cool water hold me in its grip and then swim, my arms carving through the water.

I swim a hundred metres, maybe more, back and forth across the shore in front of Fee. It's freezing, and I shiver as I wade to shore. She gives me her hoodie to wrap around my shoulders as we walk back to the caravan park.

'Proud of you,' she says as we walk back. 'I knew you could do it.'

I can't believe it. It makes me think, what else have I said no to? What else have I steered away from because I was scared?

'What about what happened to Ronnie though?' I say. 'What if they're still guarding the waters?'

Fee shakes her head.

'I've been watching them. Some nights I come and sit out here, I see their lights. They are there sometimes, but not always. There's a shift change at night, sometimes the second boat doesn't come for an hour. I say we go silently, and we go at night. We have to try, Jay.'

'We have to try,' I agree.

'What about Kit? I told him I'd never leave him.'

She pauses for a moment.

'Then Kit comes too.'

'Ok.' I nod and there is a fire of adrenaline in my chest.

'We'll leave tomorrow night. That gives us a day to prepare.'

I turn to her and look in those grey eyes, so full of flight, of need.

'We can't tell anyone, they won't understand.'

I nod.

46

———

JAY

Saturday 26th February 2022

EARLY IN THE MORNING, before the meeting, I take a rucksack stuffed with blankets and clothes down to the shore. I hide it under Nan's decking. I fill two, five litre bottles with water from her tap. I bring ten cans of mackerel. We've had it so often that we don't care how it tastes now. I find three life jackets that Nan used to keep under her deck.

I feel guilty not saying anything to Robin but what good will it do? We have to go. I scribble a note to him and leave it in my caravan. If he comes looking, he'll find it.

'Mate, I'm sorry. Fee's sick – we've gone to get help.'

I wake Kit at midnight and carry him, still warm with sleep, down to the shore. We set off in the dark which is the safest way.

As we row quietly away from the island, Kit lies low in

the boat, now awake and watching the black water for flash-lights, for clues. There's no one there.

I row on and on, and I expect a shot in the back of my neck with every stroke. Fee is too weak to help. There is no one to stop us, only our own fear. It makes me wonder why we didn't try it sooner, and then it strikes me, that perhaps we didn't really want to leave. All we have is a map and a compass and hope in a miracle.

Setting off in Lily's rickety old boat, it feels like death is right there with us, lying right alongside Fee. I have never seen her weak like this. I can see she's scared.

'These birds you talked about,' I whisper. 'Can't you call them, say that you need help? Do they know what we're doing?'

'It's not like that. You can't just call them,' she laughs, as she lies down on the floor of the boat, and we float out into the black arms of the sea. 'I guess they know, though. I only became a changeling the day the birds came. I didn't have any control over it. I was just watching them, on the pier at Southend, and I had a heart full of longing to get here.'

'You were the start of the chain,' I say. 'The place where it started.'

I think back to that day. Me being scared shitless of that black lake. Scared of Swanny and his bravado too.

'What's so special about me?' Fee shrugs.

Who would think that nine months later, I'd be rowing out across the channel with this girl that I love, who is dying right here on the floor of this boat, and with Kit, this skinny boy who has turned up in my life demanding that I love him too? I'm terrified of death, and here it is, sidling right up to me, sitting right here with us all. I think of Mum, this unending sea, and the way Kit has swerved death and found a new life. And now here we are, heading into open water in a rowing boat. Its freezing and we wear our winter coats and gloves. Fee and Kit try to sleep as I row through the black night.

We don't know what will happen when we get to shore, only that there is no other choice.

Robin will take care of the kids until we get back. He'll wake up and find the note. He'll tell the others we've gone. They'll say we're selfish, that we've given up on the island. But really, I'm just trying to save the ones I love.

Love gives you a fuel in the belly that you've never known before. It drives you to do the unimaginable.

THERE IS near silence in the boat as the light breaks. It's unspeakably beautiful. The water is like a millpond, and Lily's boat carries us like pearls in an oyster. Fee is napping under my jacket. Her lips are parched. She drinks and drinks. She eats a little, sleeps a little, has half her strength. I try to play games with Kit in the boat, but he feels sick, so mostly there is silence. I just keep rowing, trying not to think about the depth of the water underneath our boat. I relax a little as the day dawns.

'Migration,' murmurs Fee, shifting and sitting up. 'The birds woke us up to it, to the new way that we are going to have to live now.'

She trails her hand in the water.

'Like scavengers, moving over the face of the earth. We will have to find what is left, to bide our time.'

'Before...' I ask.

She shrugs.

'What if this is the beginning of the end? Maybe the birds have come to tell us that the way we live needs to change – that we need to live the way *they* live. What if we all just need to live wandering now?'

'The UK is broken, it's true. I don't know how we'll ever get back from it.'

'Trade turns us all into animals,' Fee says. 'We are held in a balance so fine, that when it tips, we all know about it. We are slaves to the global system. Truly, none of us can be free. Only the birds.'

The water laps against the boat as I pull the oars.

'Your mum was circling around you, that's how I knew … that she was your Mum, I mean.'

I just stare at her.

'You really think my Mum is a bird now. Why didn't she tell me?'

'That might have been difficult,' she says.

'So, what, do they look like birds or people?'

'I can't explain it, I can sense their faces, but they still look like birds. I guess it's like a second sight. I don't know.'

She closes her eyes.

Kit is still sleeping, his lifejacket hunched up around his shoulders, his winter coat over him like a blanket.

'TIME IS RUNNING OUT,' Fee says to me. She looks at me with an urgency I hadn't seen before.

'Are you ok?' I ask.

'Not me, the birds. They're closing in. The birds are coming back, I know it, I can feel it. And what if this time it's for us? I think they're trying to save us from the EFR. But I need to know what's happened to Dad first. We need to tell him what's happening on Sheppey. I don't even care if I die any more. I just need to get there.'

Monday 28th February 2022
The Channel

Silence is the way
between that world and this.
A bridge between the world we have created,
small but surviving, and the other one, outside.
What will it be like if we make it?
What will it be like on the other side?
If I will my body strength, if I do not let myself die,
will I be able to get there?
How can I be a bird and be so frail?
Will they help me?
Will they hear me if I call?

48

FEE

Monday 28th February 2022
Dunkirk

We row through a night and then, miracle of miracles, the land comes into view.

We pull the boat up on to an empty beach at first light and walk into the town. We stumble through the streets in a daze. We buy a baguette and fresh water and eat noisily. Everyone around us looks so well-fed and relaxed. Kit seems disgusted by it.

'Don't they know what's going on?' he whispers.

We shush him and keep walking.

At the nearest hospital, I speak in French, repeat the lines that I'd practiced with my father.

'I am staying with my aunt in Dunkirk. I have run out of insulin and need an emergency prescription. Can I take it today?'

They don't put me on a drip, don't ask too many questions. They just hand the emergency prescription to me in a clear plastic bag, and I want to hug them so hard. They have saved my life.

After that, we find a quiet part of the beach. I need to rest. My ketones are still high, which gives me a raging headache and thirst, but after I inject the cool insulin, my sugars slowly come down, and my body can work the way it is meant to. We hide in the dunes while I recover. It takes a whole day to bring the ketones down. I have to rest while the insulin does its work in my body, and drink to flush the ketones out.

BY THE EVENING I am feeling slightly better and the safe house in Belgium is calling. It's near Ostend, so it would be easier to get the train but it's too hard to go unnoticed because of the border. It is a ten hour walk if Kit doesn't slow us down too much. We start out after dinner and walk along the coast and through the fields. We cross the border at night through farmland, sleep in a hedgerow for a few hours, our coats wrapped around us. We wake as soon as the light peeps over the horizon and we get there before dark that night.

I've been there before, before they shut the seas. I had memorised it. Papa had told me years ago. Out on the road to Gistel, left at the farm, right after the old church and follow the track until you find the farmhouse. He said to store it in my memory where no one could take it from me.

We walk right up to the door my father said to come to, early in the morning. Jay carries Kit as he dozes. I recognise the house as if from my dreams. It's an old farmhouse, the walls forming a U-shape around a courtyard. There is a green door, slightly ajar, a cat curled up in the sun in the courtyard.

'Bonjour?' I call in through the doorway. 'Il y a quelqu'un?'

And there is silence for a while, but then the shuffling of feet and the oldest of men appears from the darkness. He wears a flat cap and slippers. He walks with a stick and his eyes are shrunken into his folds of skin and seem to shy from the light.

'Oui, mademoiselle?'

'C'est Paul?' I ask, unsure. 'Je cherche mon pere.'

'You are his daughter,' he says. 'You look like him.'

'Papa n'est pas la?'

'No,' he explains. 'They took him away.'

And my heart can't take any more of it. All this way, all that waiting, all that journeying to find him. And he isn't here.

'Who is "they"?'

'The authorities, you know. They knew he was working for the UK.'

Paul makes us bowls of coffee and we sit in his shady kitchen, eating baguettes with strawberry jam, dipped into our coffee. It is a meal from heaven. He explains in heavily accented English, 'Your father was taken away, because they feared he was part of the resistance, which he was. So, to prove his 'fidelity' to the French government, he is working for them, assessing the effect of the Cut Off on the economy, trying to do his best to put forward reasons why France should open the seas again. You and your mother being the first reason. He is in Paris now. If you go to him, and say you have an appointment about "the sustainability of the seas," he will know it's about the resistance.'

We stay with Paul for a few days. It is the first time we've been safe for months and we all need to rest. I sleep and sleep and sleep. Kit plays with the cat and Paul shows him around the farm.

Two days later, Paul drives us as far as he can, and leaves us in a field on the outskirts of Paris. We will have to do the rest on foot.

'This is as far as I can safely get you,' he says. 'I am on their radar too.' We thank him and set off again, back to the eye of the storm. We get an early train into the city, say nothing, pay in cash, tell Kit to keep quiet.

First things first, if I'm going to have a meeting, I need to have something to wear.

I call from a payphone.

'I need to speak with Jonathan Etourneau,' I say, in my shaky voice. Although I'm fluent, I still feel sure they will catch me out.

And then Papa's voice is on the line, and I tremble as I speak, and everything in me wants to whisper 'Papa,' but the lines are bugged, and I know I can't trust anyone.

'I need to speak with you about the sustainability of the seas,' I say. 'It must be this week; it is an urgent matter.'

He says, 'Certainly, I can see you today. You want to come to the office?'

I say yes and hang up. I don't think he realises it's me.

Into the mouth of the beast, I go.

Dad had left me 400 euros for my emergency fund. Having already bought the train tickets and food, there is still enough to buy something to wear, so I don't look out of place. There is a boutique not far from his office and I pick up trousers and a jacket and then pull my hair into a ponytail in the changing room. I give my tatty rucksack to Jay and they wait in a park across the street. I try to be confident as I walk into his office, but I feel sick. Surely, they will catch me out. He has a glass office, and I see his face fall with shock as he sees me approach his desk. He hadn't recognised my voice.

'Fee,' he says, as the secretary brings me to his room. He must keep up the pretence, pretend I'm just a colleague. People are watching.

We sit down and I long to hug him, touch his hand, but I can't.

'Papa,' I mouthed to him. 'I almost died.'

'Come,' he says, and he picks up his coat. 'We will go for lunch.'

He takes my arm, and we duck out of the office and into a

Parisian street. It is busy and I follow my father as he swerves up side streets and into a park. We sit on a bench together.

'This is the safest we'll be,' he whispers. 'Fee, I've missed you so much. How is your mother?'

'I don't know. Have you heard about Sheppey? I went there – I was trying to get to you. I can't explain it, it's like I was called there, but that same night I arrived, the birds came, and all the adults disappeared.' I tell him everything that has happened since September. 'Can you help them, Papa? I haven't seen Mum since last September. She doesn't even know where I am.'

'Oh, my darling Fee. I've heard nothing. We must speak out, for the sake of the kids. But that puts you in danger. I could say I got an anonymous tip-off, but you need safe passage back to the UK. Or I pretend I don't know you, that you have just arrived here.'

'Yes,' I say. 'Pretend we don't know each other. But how long will it be until I see you again?'

He shrugs.

'I love you,' I say, and I reach over and squeeze his hand.

I follow him back to the office where he nods and picks up the phone, in full acting mode now.

'There is a UK whistle-blower in my office who needs to be deported immediately ... I don't know how she got to the EFR ... The UK government are covering up a catastrophe ... I don't care if we have no jurisdiction. We have to care because these are children who have been left to die.'

He slams down the phone with tears in his eyes.

'It is not like it was, when we cared for children whatever their nationality. They say we can't help you.'

He sits down.

Minutes later, the police come and drag me away.

'There are others outside,' I say.

If I am being deported, I need Jay and Kit to be deported with me.

Papa can't keep his cover, though. As they drag me roughly, away from his office, my feet stumbling, he calls out, 'Fee,' and runs to me to embrace me once more.

'Papa,' I whisper, fear in my eyes. I thought he was stronger than this.

And in my ear, the tiniest of whispers, 'They are coming. Tell the PM.' And then he says, in a softer voice, 'I love you.'

I don't know what his fate will be now.

But I have been held by him again, and that is all I've dreamed of, for years.

49

JAY

F riday 4th March 2022
    Paris

THEY AREN'T SO unkind to me, Fee and Kit. The French police push us into cars, and then onto a chartered boat. A quick hop back across the channel and they deposit us into the hands of the authorities at Dover.

Home again. Home to the mainland. Except we haven't set foot here since the birds came and it's not home, is it? Not now.

We've made it, but I don't feel the elation I expected. At the port, there is a heavy presence of armoured soldiers. I feel blindsided by the sight of the citizens – their heads hanging low, their faces grey.

Border control take us for questioning in a portacabin in Dover. Two plain faced, middle-aged men welcome us in from the rain, and offer us a cuppa.

'So where are you from, then?' one officer asks, in a cockney accent. 'Brave, int you, to row across the Channel?'

'We're from Sheppey,' I answer.

They look at each other, shift a little on their seats.

'Sheppey? Where the accident happened?'

'What accident?' I say, wondering what it is that they think they know.

'The nuclear power station up at Sheerness.'

We look at them blankly.

'There was a toxic radiation blast, no survivors. The whole island is a contamination zone – no-one's set foot on there for months.'

'We live there. With all the other kids. They left us behind. There was no explosion. We just woke up one day and all the adults had gone, that's all.'

They look at each other, confusion in their eyes, and then back at us three.

'Nah. You're having us on,' the older one says, with concern in his eyes. He wants it to be a lie. 'It was all over the news, I saw the pictures. That island's a massive exclusion zone.'

'Is that what you've been told?' says Fee. 'What did the French authorities tell you?'

'They said some kids got across the channel.'

'From Sheppey.'

'They didn't mention the island.'

'But we were the whistleblowers,' says Fee. 'We just risked our lives to get there. I may have cost my dad his life.'

'I don't know nothing about whistleblowers,' says the officer.

'The army know! They were guarding the bridge. They said they'd shoot us if we tried to leave,' says Fee.

'We're just kids,' I murmur, to myself. I stand up, and

pace around the portacabin in frustration. 'No one listens to us.'

'You have to help them,' says Kit, quietly. 'They're gonna run out of food.'

Kit's small voice spurs me on. 'We swear to you. There are hundreds of children stuck there. We were told we couldn't leave, an armed soldier said we couldn't go. They ... they shot one of our friends on the bridge. He was trying to cross.'

'But it's deserted. No one's been there for months.'

'Fuck's sake, there are children there, I'm telling you now.'

'Who's running this operation?' interjects Fee.

The men look at each other blankly.

'Take us there now,' I say. 'We'll show you.'

They falter and I know that they can see that the pain in our faces is because we're telling the truth.

TWO DAYS LATER, we are escorted to the bridge by one of the men from the portacabin and his Chief Inspector. They stop at the bridge and change into hazmat suits and masks. We come as we are. There is still one soldier guarding the bridge now. I guess the kids have given up trying to come this way. We sit in the back of the police car while the police officers speak with him.

'We have intelligence that there are still kids alive on the island.'

'I'm under orders to let no one past. It is a nuclear exclusion zone. No one's been in or out for six months.'

'I don't care. I am a Chief Inspector, and you will open this bridge now.'

The lad kind of looks like he can't be arsed anymore. He

looks both ways and then says, 'Ok, fine, but you won't find anything. Like I said, they're all dead. But if you want to go risking your life then go ahead.'

He goes ahead and pulls the coils of barbed wire out of the way to make a path. Swanny's mum's car is still there, the window screen shot in. Will's body has been moved. For some reason, I look for the stain on the tarmac but can't make it out.

We cut across the barren land, not a soul in sight. The grass has come up at points through the tarmac. The whole place is empty and palatial. It is slowly regreening itself in the quietness.

As we approach Leysdown Holiday park, I suddenly feel sick to the stomach. There is no way to forewarn them all. What if they don't want to be rescued?

We stop next to the burned-out shell of Pete's place. I get out, and then remember I am not free, and this is not my home anymore.

The children have gathered on the green, drawn by the foreign sound of engines, I guess. We only left a few days ago but it seems that everything is different now. It's Robin's eyes that I look for first.

'I wanted to tell you,' I say. 'Fee was dying. She's diabetic and she ran out of medicine. So we did the craziest thing, we took a boat and we crossed the channel. We wanted you to be safe.'

'It's ok,' he says, and I believe him.

And though I think they understand that this couldn't have gone on forever, there are still searching eyes and downcast gazes. Because there is no home if not this. There are no parents left to make a home. What home can there possibly be?

Standing there on the other side, the adults' side, I can

see how dirty they look, how small, how sad. This couldn't have gone on forever, could it? The enormity of what we have just done engulfs me and my ears begin to throb. I sit down on the ground.

The kids in front of us are quiet, wondering what next. I wonder who the leader is now. I turn to the border control man, and the Chief Inspector, so dressed up in protective gear that I can only see their eyes and I say, 'We told you.'

They are speechless.

'They knew we were here,' I say. 'There were soldiers on the bridge. They told us we couldn't leave. We told them we'd die, and they didn't care, they just turned their backs on us. It was months ago.'

'They killed my brother Will,' comes a voice, sharp like a dagger from the back. Leah. 'Shot him as he ran to them.'

There is a pause for air and then the border control guy takes charge.

'Ok, ok,' one of them says, his hands up as if in surrender. 'It's all over, you're safe now. We're gonna take you home.'

His words ring with emptiness. Nothing's over, we're not safe. This is home, we haven't got any other place to go.

But we're tired too, and it's easier to let them be adults.

Just then, I hear the sound of more vehicles. There is a convoy of army trucks and unmarked vans. The vehicles screech to a halt and the soldiers pile out at once. They seem to form a circle around the police officers who are then shoved into the back of one of the vans. I get a funny feeling in my stomach. Something isn't right. This isn't how our rescue was supposed to look.

A woman gets out, wearing a smart suit. She looks completely out of place. She looks around, gives nothing away on her face. There are some sort of paramedics, although they're wearing odd uniforms. No one wears any protective clothing. They ask us to form a queue. They hand out bottles of water, and do vitals checks on every child.

Our child hearts are pushed down again as soon as these adults arrive, and I feel I have failed the kids. We all grow down and unlearn the last six months. Just like that.

But what was I supposed to do? Call to someone? God? The king of the starlings? I had to save Fee, didn't I? I had to keep her safe.

Hours later, after they have checked everyone over, we are loaded into the unmarked vans. I didn't see what happened to the police officers.

'Will we come back again?' asks Sienna, one of the girls.

'No, we're going find you new homes,' says one of the nurses, a small smile on her face.

Sienna looks from side to side, and then takes the hand of the girl next to her.

The kids board the buses quietly. Fee and I are on the front row and as we pull away, I turn to see their faces all pressed to the windows to get a final glimpse of home.

50

JAY

S aturday 5th March 2022
Kent

THE VANS TAKE us to a detention centre, which seems completely empty apart from us. Its grey concrete mass looks and feels like a prison. The woman in the suit is a constant presence. The staff take our clothes, shower us, and give us new overalls to wear. We are to be decontaminated, quarantined for thirty days, and examined, they say. They take all our things from us, our possessions, our freedom. We belong to the state now. Orphans. They test our blood, scan our brains, give us lie detector tests. Of course, they find nothing, no trace of the nuclear contamination that the border police spoke of.

In the meantime, we get to be kids again. There is TV, there is food. More food than we have seen for six months. Creamy mash and chicken. Gravy and peas. Ok so it's still kind of like school dinners but I could cry, sitting down to plenty. Being cooked for.

The days begin with showers. Then some of us are taken for medical testing, which is different stuff each day - sight tests, blood tests, lie detector tests and other stuff, while the others sit around talking to each other. There is no contact with the outside world. There is no news, no internet. There are kids DVDs on repeat, which occupies some of the younger ones. We eat our meals in a large atrium that feels like a beehive. It has large wooden panels in abstract shapes hung around the walls. I try to talk to Robin in the cafeteria, but I keep saying the same thing because I don't have anything else to say. I did it to save us, I start by saying, or I had to save Fee too, or that we couldn't tell him any other way, but I know he feels betrayed. There is a distance between us.

The team give us counselling, tell us there was an awful accident, a radiation blast at the power plant up at Sheerness. The government barricaded the island to form an exclusion zone. It's too dangerous to live there now. There are no survivors.

Funny how when you're told something that you know to be a lie, you can end up believing it. There had to be some official narrative though, didn't there? There had to be some story. Adults don't just vanish into thin air. They had to come up with something.

Dr Brazendale, the woman who wears the suit, gathers us all in the atrium. She tells us that we were never on the island. She says we will have to sign agreements before we can leave. They will give us cash pay-outs, she says, assuming we stick to the rules.

'No one will believe you if you say you're from the island. The timeline of events has been altered. You will be transferred back to a secure facility if you ever speak of the island again. Is that clear?'

I've never been sat face to face with an adult openly lying. It's absurd. She is trying to persuade a whole room full of us that we were not on the island, that we have never been to Sheppey.

But we are not murderers, we are not liars. Something happened to our parents, and it cannot be explained. We have suffered the biggest loss, and here they are, trying to rewrite the past. It astounds me that they think they'll get away with this.

'How can you say this?' I say. 'You know we were on the island.'

'Jay, that is not an appropriate response. You will not speak of the island.'

But even as she said it, I can see a wavering in her eyes.

'Don't you want to know what really happened? Don't you want to hear what we have to say?'

I thought things couldn't get much more screwed up than life on the island, but it turned out I was wrong.

She doesn't respond but reaches down to press a buzzer on the podium in front of her and two men in dark clothes escort me swiftly out of the room. They take me to a smaller room, bare apart from a table and two chairs.

I wait for what seems like hours, but then Dr Brazendale comes in and sits down opposite me.

'The thing is, Jay, we can't have you ruining things for everybody else. These children are traumatized. They need to be able to heal, to integrate into a new family. They don't need to be confused about your version of what may or may not have happened.'

'But I'm telling the truth.'

'But Jay, what is the truth? There were no survivors.'

She smiles a sickly-sweet smile and stands up to leave.

DESPITE THE BRAINWASHING, it's strangely calming to be there at the centre, to be safe, to be clean, to have beds to sleep in. It's not your typical rescue, none of us have homes to go to. They say we are safe now, but we trust no one and have nothing. There is no real sense of relief.

There is time, though, and the kids are safe, so today I walk past Fee in the breakfast queue, grab her hand, and we walk back to my room. No one notices us leave the main hall. I lock the door behind us as we sit there on the bed, in the quiet. It is the first time we have been alone in so long. It is the first time we are not responsible for the lives of others.

'I was just wondering how you feel about us, now that you're safe again, now that we're not responsible for all those kids?'

She looks at me quizzically.

'I don't want to force you into anything if you're not ready, but you and I are pretty good together ... don't you think?'

She smiles and leans over to me.

I don't care if she's half-bird or what, but I want her now.

She kisses me, soft and full and I am happier to be alive than I ever have been. If it was all for this, it was worth it.

WE LOSE COUNT of the days that we hang around in the cafeteria/beehive and people come and go, watching us suspiciously. I try to keep track. By now, no one is wearing protective clothing, but I can see the staff are still wary of us.

One day there is a meeting, and Mrs Brazendale begins to talk to us of finding new homes for us all.

A few days later, when the first ones start to leave, we realise that this is it, and we won't be together anymore. Each day our numbers dwindle.

By some miracle, the authorities let Fee, Kit and I stay together. Dr Brazendale allows it but not without a threat.

'You know the rules. There was no island. You have never set foot on Sheppey. If you break them, we break you.'

They know we won't speak up; we've got too much to lose. We are assigned a flat in Clapham. We have no way to contact the other kids.

When they let us out, the acid sun sears our eyes. We have been inside for fifty days.

51

———

FEE

M onday 11th April 2022
London

PAPA TOLD me to warn the government about the EFR, and I go, as soon as I can, after the quarantine is over.

I wait outside the gates of Ten Downing Street and say I have a message for the PM. Of course, the police officers laugh at me.

'It is important, I really must speak with the PM,' I say, and they say: 'Run along little girl.'

So, I run from them and when I am out of sight, I boil with rage and burst into feathers and sinew. I fly right up to his room, through the open window and land on his desk. I look him in the eye with my iridescence and all of my power, drop the note on his desk and stay until he reads it.

'The EFR are coming.'

And then I leave, the way I had come in, through the open window, and the whole of London spreads out beneath me.

Whether or not he chooses to believe the message, well, that is up to him.

I have passed on the message from my father, like I said I would. And it makes me realise a thing. That perhaps the catalyst is rage. Perhaps that is what causes flight, these feathers, this freedom.

52

JAY

Friday 10th June 2022
London

I TURN the key in the lock to my building and can feel the weight of something on the mat as I try to push open the door. I shove it open a bit more and poke my head through the gap to see what it is.

There's a large brown envelope on the doormat. It says 'Her Majesty's Government' on the front in red type. I bend myself down around the door to pick it up – for some reason, it fills me with dread mixed with the tiniest shimmer of excitement. I tuck the envelope under my arm and climb the narrow stairwell to the flat.

I chuck my keys on the side in the kitchen, turn on the kettle, and tear open the envelope. I read aloud parts of the letter inside.

'Her Majesty's Government request a voice confession ... A testimony of your life up to this point ... In this highly unusual case, we are contacting every Sheppey survivor and asking them to tell us everything they can remember. Anything that could prevent this from happening again. You are at liberty to reveal anything at all that will help us in our enquiries.

Think about these things:

What was life like before?

What happened on the island?

Where is your life taking you now?

If you choose not to respond to this letter, we will send a representative and you will be able to make your statement in person. Please note, any non-disclosure agreements are waived for the purpose of this voice recording. You may speak freely.

You are reminded, however, that you must not speak to anyone else about what happened on the island.

You were never on Sheppey.'

I don't know what I expected to find but I have been waiting for something. Seeing it all there in black and white lights a fire in me. I screw up the letter in my fist, balling it up as tight as it will go and then let it drop to the floor.

They said it would be different now we were rehomed.

They said we would have voices.

But then they paid for our silence with their dirty money, and they separated us because we were like the birds now; we were the ones set free, and as every starling knows, its power is in the multitude. They were scared of us, I knew it. They thought that they could make us forget our truth if we didn't have each other to remind us of it. But we will never forget. It is how we were reborn, and how we learned to live.

As I stand there seething, there's a part of me that's tempted to give them what they want. A part that is being seduced so quickly by the notion of being heard, even if it's just by them. It is all I've ever wanted.

And although I'm reeling with rage and with loss, I know it will be cathartic to speak it all out, once and for all. I know what I have to say, I've been rehearsing it for three months, but why should I trust the government after what they did to us all? After they blackmailed us, separated us, paid for our silence?

I've waited long enough to speak. I will defend Kit with my life, but I can't keep this in any longer. How dare they think they can silence us all and get away with it? How dare they think that we still believe that lie, that we have nothing to say, that no one will take us seriously, because we're just kids?

I STAND THERE for a good ten minutes staring at the blank wall, letting my rage settle. And then I do it anyway, I can't help myself. I press record on voice notes on my phone.

I speak for everyone who is lost, everyone who no longer has a voice.

I speak for everyone who became one of us.

I start in bits and pieces. I talk a lot. There is so much to say.

Maybe they will listen this time.

'VOICE CONFESSION #1, *Jay Fisk. Sheppey survivor.*

LET *me go back to the beginning.*

·　·　·

IF YOU WERE BORN on the island, you didn't look up at the horizon.
    Across the sea or in your own life.
    No point, you'd say.
    In fact, there was no point even thinking there was no point.
    If you thought it, it made you miserable,
    so instead you took delight in getting your measly pay cheque
    and trotting down the shop to get yourself a scratch card.
    Knew you'd never win, did it anyway.
    You worked in the manky holiday shops,
    selling overpriced buckets and spades to gullible Londoners,
    or heart-attack chips for the Saturday night lovers.
    Either that or you worked in the prisons,
    the grey, pulsating heart of the island,
    and it made you think that anyone breathing this island air
    was a prisoner of some kind.
    You enjoyed the Friday night quiz night down the Black Dog,
    and even the greasy chips at sundown on the front on a
Saturday
    with the weekenders from London, and the wanderers
    down to visit their beloved ones in the clink.
    Made you feel part of something,
    but when the winter closed in and the darkness
    pinned the place down even tighter,
    it was another matter.
    You still kind of enjoyed the sea, the sunsets,
    but they were pretty samey,
    so, you tended to waddle back to the holiday park
    and crash out on the sofa with some beers and a gameshow
instead.
    Anything to not have to think anymore,
    to anaesthetise the boredom.
    You'd often fall asleep there and wake up at 3am

with some long-forgotten war movie blasting out into the dark lounge.

 The caravans got a real chill in them at night, out of season,
 so, you'd crawl into bed and fall asleep
 until the light seeped through the thin curtains
 and the chill in your shoulders pulled you back into consciousness.

AND THAT WAS IT, *until some crazy bird stuff blew up.*

ALL I DREAMT *of was leaving. For my whole life.*
 The island made me think of dead ends,
 of roads that ran around in circles.
 All the views pointed out to sea,
 and reminded me of nothingness, of being left.

THERE WAS *a bad taste in my mouth which I got from Mum.*
 It was a dissatisfaction with this life,
 not that it wasn't good enough for me here,
 not that I deserved better,
 but that I was thirsty for change.
 I was hungry to be homeless,
 to fly the nest,
 to make everywhere my home,
 the way that folks did these days.'

53

JAY

W ednesday 22nd June 2022

THE VOICE CONFESSIONS quickly become a way of life. I drop Kit off at school, Fee goes to work, and I talk. Since we've been in London, Fee has been volunteering for Child Protection Services, running workshops for resettled children.

The kids' eyes lit up the first time she walked in, she says, but they know not to give her away. If they do, they know they won't see her again.

She finds the survivors all over the city. She writes a list. She has twenty-three now out of sixty. There are some who've been rehomed elsewhere, of course, and she's learned to let those ones go. There were too many to accommodate in London, but the ones she finds, she treasures.

She looks at them as they speak, listens to what they have to say. That's the most important thing for her. Letting them have their voice. They all know the condition though: they can't talk about the island anymore. Anything else, but not that. The authorities have said so. So, Fee talks about the present, the future. Never the past.

I work from home for one of the mainland papers. I was surprised how quickly it happened once we got over here. Only junior, so I'm mostly writing up sports fixtures and checking job ads for typos. It's a start though, I tell myself. I've got my foot in the door.

We're like fish out of water in London. But this is normal life, isn't it? It's what we wanted for so long. We know it will take some time to settle.

We've started from scratch again here. I've got no photos of Mum, Dad or Zozo now. I didn't really think we'd be leaving for good when we went back, didn't really say good-bye. Guess it's all there as we left it.

But now I've only got the pictures I keep in my mind, just the memory of a sunblind selfie, taken a lifetime ago.

One thing I wasn't expecting was to see the Army on the streets of the mainland. Makes you shrink inside yourself a bit more. People say they appeared after the Cut Off riots. We didn't really see them on Sheppey, but on mainland, it went wild by all accounts. Then that September, when the birds came, things went downhill even more over here. No medicines, no jobs. Folks got angry and the troops helped to bang them into a bit of compliance. That's what we've been told. People look weaker now after so long living on rations. Tins and food that keeps for years. Not a lot of fruit and veg about. Not in London anyway. People look tired. Tired of the troops, of being kept in line. They look broken.

London isn't what I imagined, but at least I've kept my promise to Mum – the one that I made all those years ago; that makes sense deep inside me, and I hope she sees it somehow. I got off the island. I'm here, like I said I'd be, and I wonder if she's here too somewhere, under the same London sky.

What if Fee is mistaken? What if Mum isn't a bird but is still alive somewhere? What if she could change back again? What if she could give me a real hug again and I could smell her, her warmth, her perfume tinged with cigarette smoke?

She could meet Kit and Fee. She'd never believe any of it. She'd be so proud of me.

I DIDN'T KNOW what it was to love someone before Kit. Even with Zozo. I just took her for granted. But with Kit, I saw his aching need that time at the playground, and the bottom fell out of my heart, and there was more room there, somehow.

Kit reminds me of Zoe, the way he roars with laughter at the smallest of things, the way he wakes with a smile on his face, even after everything.

As I drop him off at school each morning, and I can't help but think about Mum, the way she used to plant a kiss on top of my head when she said goodbye.

And so, I do it for Kit too. I tell him I love him more than anything and give him a squeeze as I wave goodbye. I wonder where the love has all come from and realise that all my words and all my affection come from Mum and the way she loved me.

She taught me that love has hands: that it washes you, holds you, comforts you. So that is what I show Kit. It's weird, suddenly being his guardian, all official. Weird how the authorities have let us get away with it. But it means they have a bargaining chip, doesn't it? They know how much it means to us that Kit stays with us. They know we'll do anything to keep it that way. Even stay silent? Not today.

Sometimes me and Fee can't believe our luck. Sometimes it doesn't sit right. None of it makes sense. London. The EFR. Surviving.

Because what's next for us? Will we learn to fit in and forget everything the island has taught us? What was the point of it all?

We feel stifled, being inside all the time. We feel trapped, having to turn up to jobs on time, having to buy food in plastic boxes, not having any space to grow things. The air smells of overstuffed bins, petrol, cigarettes.

Where is the salty sea breeze? Where's the deep scent of grass that you can breathe right down into your lungs? Where's the rush of the sea, stilling your anxiety, carrying it away?

We miss the kids, the island, the birds.

Those London dreams don't seem to be what I need anymore.

We're here, but it's not what we thought it would be.

Fee is anxious. Being off the island has changed her. It has clipped her wings, but at least we're safe. She doesn't talk much about the bird thing anymore and I've filed it under unexplainable perhaps delusional. To be fair, though, what right do I have to say I don't believe her when our parents vanished into thin air?

I wonder why I still have this nagging sense of unease, though. I can't escape the feeling of sorrow in my chest, like something vital has been lost.

Nights, Fee sits by the window, her legs folded up in front of her, making herself as small as she can. I can tell she feels uneasy here. I'm not sure if it's the noise, the closeness of everything, the sudden change, or seeing her father again. Maybe it will just take us a while to get back to normal.

In a way we think we are radicals, in a way we are still minions, trying to find our place in the machine. We can't tell which, but it seems no one wants much to do with us now, only for us to slot into the same ruts that everyone else is mindlessly following.

'What would you do though,' we sometimes ask each other, 'if you could go anywhere? Where would you go?'

Always dreaming of freedom.

'I'd go west,' she always says. 'Down to the rugged beaches. Not so many people.'

'Yeah, I think I'd go west too, towards the sun,' I say, thinking I wouldn't want to be anywhere where she isn't.

Kit is asking questions again. He goes quiet on it for weeks, and then it gets to him again, as it would to anyone.

'But what *actually* happened to my Aunty?' he says, and we reassure him, saying: 'Kit, you're safe now, remember? It won't happen again', but he doesn't always buy it, and the truth is, how do we know?

We don't know what happened to his Aunty. All we know is that she disappeared. How do I know that the land we're walking on isn't as thin as ice? How do we know the birds, or someone else, won't come back for us? How do we know we aren't being watched?

The thing we lived through made everything around us seem unstable, close to breaking. It felt as if all of this was a film set, unreal, somehow.

We have questions all the time, but with the way they split us all up, Fee and I only have each other and Kit to talk to. We haven't seen Swanny and Rob since the detention centre. I miss them. Mostly Rob. Fee hasn't heard any word of Rob or Ava in her groups. Someone said that Swanny was sent up to Manchester to stay with his uncle.

We try to find Rob on the internet, but we know it's monitored. It's almost as if they think we have some sort of power.

A thought bubbles up within me for weeks, and then, laughing, I say to Fee one night, 'You know, I think they might actually be scared of us. I reckon they think we murdered the adults. Fee, the birds have given us the upper hand. The government are terrified of us.'

She looks at me, says, 'No, they can't be!' but then she goes quiet for a moment. I think she knows I am right.

54

JAY

W ednesday 18th August 2022

'Voice Confession #24, Jay Fisk, Sheppey Survivor.

On the news *they said everyone had died. They'd all been told that there was a nuclear disaster and that there were no survivors.*

The government said that they had no choice but to barricade the island completely. It was a contamination zone and everything within it was already dead.

Driving back there, with the Border Police, the Chief Inspector asked me, 'What happened to the bodies?' through his hazmat suit.

They talked of searching the island, as if we'd murdered them but we told them over and over that they'd find nothing.

There are still mysteries. I never could tell whether Fee was telling the truth. Perhaps her illness confused her, maybe she was hallucinating. Could the adults really have turned to birds? Did she really see Mum? All I know is that the adults all disappeared and the starling population over Sheppey soared.

Fee has never been up with the birds since. Perhaps it was the trauma that made her imagine she could fly, that made her imagine she saw my Mum, but there's one thing I can't figure out. If she made it all up, how did she get to the island in the first place? And how did she know my mum had disappeared? We don't talk about it now. It rests between us, silently, like so much else.

Let the children speak, I have thought, so many times, and now it is a drum inside my heart. So, when you tell me I can speak freely, I will.

It must have been the prison service that notified the government. It showed up on their central CCTV. A camera, in each cell. And then, at the same time. 23.26, they all just disappeared. There was supposed to be an independent enquiry into what happened but it never started – I think the investigators were too fearful. So instead they spun their tales.

But instead of imploding emotionally, or worse still, dying, we grew hearts, we grew up, we fell in love. I'd always wondered what would happen when we were left to our own devices.'

55

JAY

Thursday 19th August 2022

WE WERE TOLD *that no one would ever believe us, that if we dared to speak out, people would say we had killed our parents. We were threatened with detention centres. And after what we'd been through, that was the only thing they could threaten – we'd already lost everything else.*

But we knew what was true. We spoke about it, remembered it, and it lit a fire within us. The fire stoked the rage, and the rage would have to be let out, sometime. We knew it was coming.

I remember the first few days and months. We were reeling, going over and over it. Trawling the newspapers and the internet for reports, however small, but it was almost as if the island had been excommunicated from the country, as if that many people could just disappear.

The papers still peddled the same old story – a nuclear disaster. But it was only us kids that knew that they didn't have a clue what had happened. They had just lost three prisons-worth of inmates and 32,000 adults, and they were trying to brush it under the carpet. There was actual footage of the blast on the internet. AI generated. Fooled a whole nation.

AND THEN, one night in May, when I was trawling the internet, I found it: Elsie's blog. It all flooded back to me. Sceapig: I'd seen it on her computer that day in her house. I'd taken the photo, but my phone was taken away in the detention centre. It was her story: the unloved girl who ran away and found her home down there with the birds. The birds had marked her out; she had known they were coming back. This is what she wrote:

'ELSIE LAY in the long grass of her parents' home, hiding from everything but the birds. Her folks kept up the pretence of marriage for someone, but she wasn't sure who. There was hardly any love in that house. She quickly learned that hiding was the only way to survive.

When she was eight, she had walked into the police station and said, "I don't wish to live with my mother and father anymore; they don't want me. Is there somewhere else I can go?"

The police officer roared with laughter and took her straight back home. Her heart sank as she realised that no amount of reasoning or politeness would get her away from there, and that the only thing to do was last it out and sink into her own world until she was old enough to leave.

As she lay there looking up at the bright blue sky and the swirling clouds, a starling swooped down and landed on her chest. Its feathers shone with the swirling colours of an oil slick. It pinned her down with its tiny gripping feet. It tilted its head this way and that, looking at her.

The bird hopped a little closer, and she shielded her face with her hands, watching through her fingers. It tapped its foot on her heart, testing her for readiness, and then looked straight at her, its beady eyes shining.

"Take me with you," she whispered.

The starling pecked at her chest, with tiny pummels like a miniature pneumatic drill. She opened her mouth to scream, but she found that it didn't really hurt. It was an odd sensation – ticklish, almost.

Then it was over, and the starling flew away, its feet pushing down into her chest for take-off.

That night as she was getting ready for bed, she unbuttoned her checked shirt, looked at her chest and saw the wound, red raw down the centre.

It didn't fade with time but grew into a defiant scar, shiny and raised from the skin.

One morning, lying in bed, she felt for the scar, like she did every morning, and it came to clarity within her: "The starlings are the warning. They are marking people out". She gasped and pushed herself up onto her elbows. "They are looking for people to rescue."

She didn't know how she knew it; she just did.

She bided her time until she turned sixteen, then she ran away, skipping between friend's houses, swearing them all to secrecy.

Her parents didn't even report her as missing.

The day she turned eighteen, she sat in her flat, breathing a sigh of relief, and eating cake that she had made for herself. She had managed to get herself into uni. She was no longer beholden *to them. Eighteen and finally free. She never had to see them again if she didn't want to.*

A grateful child saw the gift that her parents' neglect had given her – independence. A reliance on no one, only her own skin and bone.

She never forgot the promise, and every night the scar reminded her.

"We are coming back! We are coming back! We are coming back!"'

SHE KNEW THEY WERE COMING. *I've often wondered if she was the one who called them to come and fix us. Because they knew how to live, and we didn't. Perhaps they had been watching us for years, making a mess of this thing we called migration; some needing to pitch up somewhere and call it home and also wanting so much to be safe, others shutting the door on them, saying, "It is my land, it is mine!"*

Perhaps they knew it was only the youngest who were malleable enough to learn to live another way, soft enough to learn to love their neighbour, no matter where they were born, or where they were trying to go.

Elsie had been waiting for so long for them to come back. And she's safe with them now. You can't touch her.

I haven't seen Rob or Swanny since the island. We said we'd keep in touch, but you've done a good job to keep us all apart. You are watching us, we know you are.

When I found Pete in his caravan, he had a line of solder down his chest too. I know it's crazy but it's my best explanation for all of this, they were testing him for readiness too. It was the birds. They took them all.'

JAY

F riday 20th August 2022

'VOICE CONFESSION #26, Jay Fisk, Sheppey Survivor.

YOU SAY REMEMBER a time before it all.
But how could I?

I WAS a boy in a boat on a lake going nowhere.
Pushed into the black lake,
scared to swim, scared to breathe.
Paralysed by my Mum leaving,
when all I really wanted to do was run away like she did.

· · ·

My world imploded a little bit more
    with each dent, each crack, each failure.
    Dad, the caravan park, the Cut Off, the birds.
    But then one day there it was, a way out.

I'd been living in a cave, and when it fell in on me,
    there was a chink of blue and I crawled towards it.
    That's all.

Do I miss Dad? Not really. I'm glad he's gone.
    Not because I didn't love him,
    I love him so hard it hurts.
    But he's with Mum now I guess, and Zoe.
    I can imagine them getting breakfast
    at an all you can eat buffet in Greece.
    Lying on sun loungers with Zozo messing about by the pool.
    Safe as houses, she is, because you can't die in heaven.

We're settled now: me, Fee, Kit.
    Leaving it all behind us.
    So much water under the bridge.
    Kit is eight now, he's in school,
    comes back with his beady eyes shining,
    ready to tell us all he's learnt.
    He's my link back home.
    The neediness in him is a tie
    and a reminder of myself when I was young.

· · ·

PEOPLE DIDN'T LOOK UP SO MUCH on Sheppey, didn't even see the fireball coming.

But what we learned, us kids, was that the important things were simple enough:

Love and be loved.

Look after each other.

Live, really live.

Look at the birds.

Don't just subsist like my dad did,

but fall in love with life.

I SOMETIMES WONDER about that day that I saw Mum in London.

Was it really her? I never knew.

But it doesn't feel like she's here anymore.

There was a tug on my heart before, and now there's nothing.

Almost as if she was a balloon pulling tight on a string,

and now the string has been cut and the tension has gone.

I hope she's found Dad and Zoe, hope she's with them at the pool.

YOU SAY you don't know if Sheppey will be resettled,

that there's too much contamination in the land, too much history,

that it might just be left to rack and ruin.

EVEN THOUGH YOU don't know what happened,

you're scared of it, the blood on your hands,

the weight of all those souls.

. . .

YOU SAY there's something in the land,
    but it was never about the land; it was about the skies.
    You won't listen to us kids, though.

YOU HAVEN'T OPENED the bridge again.
    Maybe you will one day; make a memorial or something,
    a place to watch the birds, to feel ourselves small under their
skies again.

BUT FOR NOW, it belongs to the birds,
    they came to reclaim it after all.
    Must be something they wanted.

WE ARE THE SHEPPEY SURVIVORS.
    I know the survivor's guilt. It holds sway over me.
    It says, why me, why us, when so many that were needed
went?
    All those dads and mums, Aunty Suz, Elsie, Pete, Dad.
    But I'm learning to let it go.
    Water off a duck's back, water under the bridge.

THERE'S nothing we can do about what happened now, is there?
    Just got to keep on walking.
    Just like we kept going on the island.
    Through the loneliest days and nights,
    through winter, fear, and panic,
    hoping that you would come to rescue us.
    And you did come, in the end.
    But by the time they did,

we had already rescued ourselves.'

I TWIRL this way and that on the office chair as I speak. This is it: the full circle, the final part.

I lean forward and press stop, hold the phone in my hands, listen back to it and crumble. And then, trembling, I type in the address and press 'SEND'. And as I hear the whoosh of an email sent, of the truth finally told, I sigh.

I don't send it to the government department like they asked me to, but to my boss at the newspaper. It's unthinkable that the country doesn't know there are survivors, that the ones who rehomed us also paid us off: ten grand each for our silence.

But enough is enough. And it has taken until now for me to be able to say it.

'Now what?' I ask, into the air.

The rest of my life, perhaps?

An unfurling that I haven't even been able to imagine before.

After everything, a kind of hope is stirring.

Like the marsh on a foggy morning.

When it starts to lift, the pink glow of dawn is thick and luminous all around you, a cold coat of light, the morning's halo. I can just imagine Elsie walking the sea wall, her shepherd's crook catching the light, her little dog running along in front.

Stop.

Not that life.

Another one, now.

Tarmac for the marsh.

A flat for the caravan.

Kit and Fee for Dad.

It is time to look around now though,
to lift up my head,
to imagine a new horizon.

I've waited a whole lifetime for this; to be off the island, to be away. I never imagined it would be like this, but here I am. I've broken the non-disclosure agreement, but I'm hoping that that will all be forgotten once the public know about what really happened. There will be an outcry, justice, somehow.

IT'S 2.33PM. I've got seventeen minutes before I need to leave to get Kit from school. I click my mobile off, put it down on the floor, and then get down on my hands and knees. I need to feel held. I roll onto my back and lie staring up at the ceiling of the flat, wondering what I've done. Was it stupid? Probably. Was it necessary? Yes.

The tears come again, and then the shakes.

I think for a minute of all that is lost: Zoe, Mum, Dad, Elsie, Pete, the others.

I think too of what will happen now that I have spoken, and of all that I stand to lose again. A sickly feeling rises in my belly, and I push it away.

It's out there now: my one small voice, my beacon in the darkness, my truth.

For a moment, the Cut Off doesn't even matter, the slow demotion to a developing country is still happening. The UK is still locked in and locked down, and how long it will go on for, no one knows, but I have spoken, and sometimes, just one voice makes all the difference.

The dodgy plasterwork on the ceiling is making me feel ill. I feel cried out. I feel calm. It is done, I have said every-thing that I wanted, finally got it all off my chest. I stand up and look at the clock. Time to get Kit. I slip my phone in my back pocket, walk down the stairs and out into the sunny London street, slamming the front door shut behind me.

As I walk to Kit's school, a sense of unease creeps up on me, but I can't put my finger on why. I feel like I have left something important in the flat. I look behind me and carry on walking.

57

FEE

F riday 20th August 2022

HE CALLS me on the way to school to get Kit.

'I've done it.'

'Done what?'

'Sent it to them, all of it – the truth.'

'Sent it to who?'

'The paper.'

And my heart starts to pound away, like it isn't supposed to anymore now that everything is fine. But the government, didn't they say we were under oath? Didn't they say they would split us up if we spoke out?

Jay reads my silence.

'When the media knows, they'll never dream of doing anything to us. We'll be heroes.'

'I'm not sure Jay.'

The line goes dead. It could be signal loss, but it feels too crisp. Has someone been listening in?

It will be ok. Deep breath.

I'll get the train home after the kids support group, we will cook pasta or something else bland, just the way Kit likes it. Perhaps we'll go for a walk afterwards, over in the park across the road. Everything will be ok.

I click the screen off and put the phone back in my pocket. I'm walking between meetings, up a busy Croydon street, heading back to the office before heading out to another group.

Sometimes it feels like our story has stopped in London. We are safe. We can pretend to be normal for a while, we can rest easy. But the truth is not out. We are gagged.

There will be a public enquiry, they said, into the accident on Sheppey, but they don't want to hear the truth of our voices, only their cover-up lies.

So maybe it will bring some good, this thing that Jay has done. I feel a flash of anger though. We should have talked it through, weighed up our choices. Talked about all that we stood to lose.

The island calls me back. I've too much bird in my bones to stay in the city now, too much flight in my mind to live in such a place. Some days I don't even look up anymore, and the longer I stay, the heavier my feet become. I don't want to lose it – the bird power I once had. I haven't flown in months, but I know that the power is still within me, I can feel it buzzing sometimes, when the rage boils in my chest, that I am about to tip over into flight.

As I cross the street to the office, I feel someone move at the same time as I do, someone far away, someone across the road. Being a bird turned on all my sensitivity. I'm aware of a thousand movements at once. I'm being followed. If they are on to me, they're on to Jay and Kit too.

It's busy and I duck down an alley, throw my bag into a bin and then, so soon, the lightness takes me and I'm flying high, over rooftops and skyscrapers.

I look down, and see a scurry of people, filing into the alley-way, all dressed differently, all spies, all watching. I didn't know there were so many.

They'll find my phone, but I can't do anything about that. They can pretend to be me, to get to Jay, but I have to trust him. He has a good head on his shoulders.

If I go back to the flat and he's left me a note, will I be able to read it? I'm still me, aren't I? Still Fee, the bird girl, who braved the sea just to look her father in the face again.

58

JAY

F riday 20th August 2022

WHEN KIT and I get back to the flat, the door is swinging on its hinge. My world falls away.

I broke the rules and so quickly everything is broken. The implications of what I have done unfold in my mind. So soon, so quick? I've only been gone for fifteen minutes. They must have been watching us.

We go inside and grab a small handful of clothes and money. I think about leaving a note for Fee. I grab the fridge magnets and write 'WEST' with them. I jumble it in amongst some other letters but if she's looking, she might see it. I try to call her but there is no answer.

Kit and I get the tube to Waterloo and then board a train to Exeter. I breathe a sigh of relief once we we're on the train.

I tap out a text to Fee but then think better of it. What if I'm giving myself away by contacting her? She knows my number. She can call if she needs to.

Where are we going? I don't know.

59

FEE

F riday 20th August 2022

I swoop in low through the doorway of the flat. The door is loose on its hinge and Jay and Kit are not there.

I am aware of all the movements about me. The air currents, the rain coming, the movements of a thousand all around me. I can hold it all in my feathered mind, my beady eye. I will find them.

The birds are my allies now, and they listen as I move. I find that we can read each other's minds as we fly.

I can't explain it, but it feels like this: we have a common goal. We don't need words. Our compassion mingles, we strive for the common good.

60

JAY

Friday 20th August 2022

As the train idles at Reading station, a line of soldiers march down the aisle. My heart sinks. They come from both ends of the carriage, so we're trapped. I recognise my boss from the newspaper, walking towards me with a sickening smile. My stomach lurches.

'Oh Jay,' he says. 'So naïve. So easy to fool because you were so desperate to have a voice. The Guardian is run by the EFR. By giving us your confession, you are giving us ammo against your own government, but shipping it off to the EFR first.

'Telling stories isn't as easy as you think it is. There are *always* implications, Jay. Your story won't be published. And because you've rebelled against the state, you'll lose your beloved girlfriend and your child. You should have done what they said, you should have stuck to your agreement.

Now you're going to lose everything. Oh, and I'm sure the EFR will be very interested in your girlfriend's secret powers.'

They shove us off the train, past the passengers, grumbling because their train is delayed.

What have I done?

I've lost everything. All over again. Just because I got carried away by the sound of my own voice. I should never have spoken.

I look up and see a whole bunch of starlings, making their way through the afternoon sky, flitting and shining in the light. They are heading west.

A voice inside me says *it's Fee*, and I have never been more certain of anything in my life.

I can't help but smile as we're being led from the platform, and as the soldiers mock us, saying: 'You'd better say your goodbyes then', and as they prepare to separate Kit and I, the birds turn and dive-bomb them, pecking at their eyes, scoring their soft flesh with their claws.

'Run, Kit!' I shout.

We run for all we're worth, into Reading's Friday crowds, ducking behind parked cars, running through half-empty department stores. We hide in *M&S*, in the ladies' section. I take off my shirt and swap Kit's t-shirt for another one we have in the rucksack. We head towards the red sun, grab a couple of *Greggs* sausage rolls and start the long walk, down to the west, away from the motorways, through the footpaths and fields.

61

FEE

F riday 20th August 2022

AFTER I SEE THEM ESCAPE, I fly up and find there is a song in me.

And later, in the darkness of the night I sing it and I go to all the places where I know the others are.

I call them out, in the night, in the darkness, the Sheppey survivors.

And at 3am, they file out onto quiet streets and deserted suburbs, following.

They walk fearlessly to the west, where I am calling them, the way Jay and Kit have gone before us.

62

JAY

Saturday 21st August 2022

WE START to see them in the dawn of the next day. As we walk, they emerge from tracks and laybys, villages and side streets, the kids we had been separated from.

Rob! And then, walking towards me, Fee. I don't know how we all find each other, it doesn't seem possible, but there's something magical in it, some magnetism, something in the universe that wants us to be together.

We sit at dawn in a field of stubble, in the shadow of the M5. We share our food, like we did that day on the way to the bridge, months ago.

It gives me déjà vu and makes me see something for the first time.

We are powerful. We are many. We can do this.

And then there is something in all of us that changes heart, all at once.

All of our compassion mingles, and we know it is right to turn and head back the way we came.

Green island, wild place. Let us in again. Hide us behind your barbed wire and contamination signs, in the quiet place where the birds roam free, where the tyres melt into grass, where the birds have begun to make their nests in the houses, where the reclamation has already begun.

The authorities won't know we are there. We aren't many. We will slip under the radar. They won't come for us, they are scared of us. Of the island. Of our supposed power. They don't know what the hell happened here. Nor do we but it ain't nothing bad. I mean, say we suspend belief and take what Fee says, that all the adults went to birds, its nothing sinister, nothing wrong with the place, just a strange happening. But maybe we don't know the half of nature. Maybe we need to let it be.

And now that London, the place I dreamed of for so long is not what I thought it was, I can't think of a better place to be.

Not all of them came to Fee's call, but they would have heard it, deep inside themselves. Deep down perhaps they will always wonder what they missed.

And maybe we'll stay as we are, as we were. Un-rescued and unfound. Re-hidden. Perhaps it's better that way. One day people will see that this is the way now. Back to the land, back to the quiet, back to the birds.

We don't know what the EFR are planning, or when they're coming. But we know what makes us strong.

And when a murmur begins and no one listens to it, it will grow and grow until the whole sky is filled with its noise.

·   ·   ·

THE KIDS GATHER in the soft light of a new morning.

We are buzzing with the idea of our newfound freedom. It weighs heavy and is risky, the idea of going back. No medicines, no grown-ups, no food. It's foolhardy. But we were getting there, before, weren't we? And it's better than here isn't it?

'SHIT!' Sophie shouts out, suddenly.

The orange glow of her phone screen lights her face. She is scrolling a news feed.

'Soph? Are you alright?' I ask, going over to see.

'MAN FALLS FROM SKY' reads the ribbon scrolling across the bottom of her phone screen.

Over and over on a loop, there is this grainy footage of a man falling onto the top of an apartment block in South West London. His body falls, doll-like, through the sky, his arms stretched upwards. The footage is on a loop, and we watch him fall again and again. Then there are shouts, and people running, the camera still rolling.

The security guard takes them up in the lift and leads them out onto the roof terrace. He approaches the body cautiously, afraid of what he'll find. He rolls him over, and his arm flops out sideways to the ground. He is naked.

And then the man's eyes flick open. The camera zooms in on his face. It looks puffy and tired. He has one black eye. He closes his eyes again.

'Dad', Sophie whispers.

The tears fall from her eyes, and she trembles as she holds the phone that everyone is craning around her to see.

'That's my dad.'

TO BE CONTINUED...

ACKNOWLEDGEMENTS

Huge thanks to my family (Joel, Sam, Ivy, Ben and Annie) who have allowed me to while away hundreds of hours on this manuscript. Thanks to mum and dad, Matthew and Esther, Don and Sarah, Jane, Rich and Gareth for their support and love too. Thanks to Melissa Welliver, who spotted the manuscript and accepted me as her mentee for the WriteMentor summer programme in 2021. Her advice and enthusiasm gave me much fuel for the long journey. Thanks also to Anne McNeil, who read an early copy of this manuscript and gave me her kind words and wisdom. Thanks to Liz Monument, who read a later version and gave me loads of ideas for further development and reading. Huge thanks also to Emma Read, my editor for spotting lots of tiny details that had been missed and also generally helping to tighten up the whole manuscript! I also want to thank Sophie Burdess, who took my inarticulate ideas and turned them into a book cover that I love so much, and which says all I wanted it to and more. I also want to thank all my beta readers: Hilary Thomas, Len and Cherry Howes, Jen Gale, Joel Pike and Vicky Barnes. Your insights were all invaluable! Thanks to my online writing group who have all been a fantastic bunch of cheerleaders this past year. Thanks also to Stuart White, whose Indie Authors Mentorship Programme was just the nudge I needed to actually get this book out there. Murmuration has been living and breathing in my heart since May 2019. Now it is May 2024 and it's finally alive in the world and I am so glad.

Elisabeth

If you enjoyed Murmuration, please leave me a review on
Amazon or Goodreads. Every review will help another
reader to find this book.

You can stay up to date with my new releases at
elisabethpike.co.uk

You can also sign up to my Substack at
https://substack.com/@minersbyelisabethpike
where I write about the creative life and new projects.

Thanks again for reading and look out for Murmuration 2
next year!